SOCIOPATHIC SURGEON

MITCHELL D. MILLER

Published in 2011 as Sara the Sociopathic Surgeon. Revised 2012, 2014, 2019, 2020, 2022.

Print ISBN: 978-1-61979-923-3
eBook ISBN: 978-1-62314-294-0

Library of Congress Control Number: 2022922743

Sixth edition

Published by
MHG Publishing
Port Richey, Florida

Cover by The Cover Collection

Assistant editor: Maxine Stone

Sociopath definition copyright Oxford University Press.

Visit the author's Website at mitchelldmiller.com.

What Readers Are Saying

"Sociopathic Surgeon is a medical suspense thriller that leaves readers guessing from one page to the next. This is one novel you must keep reading to see where the characters end up. Can they break the cycle of abuse, or are they destined to repeat the past with their own lives?" - Karen Almeida, Literary Titan

"The entire family is nuts! The author packs action and suspense into this book. The setting, the characterization and the plot keep you turning the pages. If you're up for a thriller, this book is for you."
- Tracey Lampley, Amazon US

"I liked this book, the whole family is nuts, I would really recommend it," - Isabella Fulton, Amazon UK

Dedication

Dedicated to my daughters.

Mitchell D. Miller

https://mitchelldmiller.com

Table of Contents

SO·CI·O·PATH

a person with a personality disorder manifesting itself in extreme antisocial attitudes and behavior and a lack of conscience.
- Oxford Dictionary

I Marry A Sociopathic Surgeon

My neighbors at the Hotel 17 were freaky, but it was convenient and cheap. A chilly Eastern wind propelled me from the entrance, encouraging me to get to work on time.

Although it was Friday, nobody on the Uptown IRT train was smiling. But the strangers weren't nasty, like an old girlfriend in the office elevator.

I slumped into my cubicle's chair and stared at my empty inbox and desk calendar. Bank executives were on a weekend retreat.

I left a note on my supervisor's desk that I was not feeling well. Instincts led me to the liquor store in Grand Central Station for two half pints of whiskey.

A swig of blended American whiskey on the downtown IRT reduced my hangover. The rest of the bottle improved my cafeteria breakfast.

One sip from the second bottle prepared me for the weekend. The Eastern wind propelled me to Mickey's Bar, on the Southeast corner of Warren and Greenwich Streets. Mickey's was the best low priced bar in lower Manhattan. Standard bar drinks cost $1.25.

Ace, the lone weekday bartender, welcomed me to an empty bar.

"Good morning, Sonny. Let's play pool before the lunch crowd gets here."

I shot pool with Ace, looking forward to three days away from interoffice memos.

A tall caucasian woman interrupted our third game to order a drink. Her Harris Tweed sports jacket complemented dark brown hair extending to her waist. She sat on a stool at the far end of the bar, and ordered Scotch on the rocks.

I bought Sara her second drink and introduced myself. Sara said she was waiting for a guy she met on Tuesday.

Office employees filled empty bar stools, but Sara did not greet anyone.

I showed her my best smile. "Would you like to smoke a joint outside?"

"Sure. I don't think my friend is coming. But I can't do anything on the street. Let's sit in my car," she said.

Sara's license plates were marked "MD." Why would a medical doctor drive to a bar? Is it ever a good idea to drive to a bar? Most Manhattan residents, including me, did not own a car.

We smoked in silence until Sara said, "Sometimes people think I am a nurse. I can't stand that."

"Is that so bad?"

Sara sucked in a deep breath, before she bellowed with the voice that called the cows to come home on her family's dairy farm.

"I am a graduate of an American medical school with high standards!"

Sara exhaled and relaxed. "I worked hard to graduate. I can't stand nurses. I love ordering them around."

She turned to face me. "I can't stand most people who claim to be Doctors. Medical Doctors are the only *real* Doctors.

Why are podiatrists, chiropractors and optometrists Doctors? They have no training. When someone gets sick in their office they send their patient to me."

Sara took a deep breath. She shouted, "Pee–aitch–dees are worse!"

Sara shook in disgust. "What did they do? They read a few books. They became Doctors by reading books! Do you think someone who reads a few books deserves to be a Doctor like me?"

Sara looked down and shook her head in dismay.

I sneaked a look to make sure my door was not locked before I shook my head.

Sara raised our despondent spirits. "Psychologists are the worst!"

I longed for the days of manual windows in case I needed a secondary escape route.

"Mental illness is awful," she said. "But it is also the easiest thing to cure. We have hundreds of teaching hospitals, full of mentally ill patients we can use for practice. Nice, safe patients. They sign papers so they can't sue you.

I wanted to be a psychiatrist. But it's a seven–year residency, and nobody gets better right away.

In surgery you're finished with a patient in two hours. In psychiatry it could take two years. I did a six–week psychiatric rotation during my internship. I loved it. Don't you think I could be a great psychiatrist?"

My biggest drinking problem was saying stupid stuff, but I was speechless. I caught myself nodding.

"Psychiatrists are real Doctors. They understand medicine. They know mental illness is a disease.

You treat diseases with drugs. When a psychiatrist asks about your family, he's only interested in your genes. Like if your parents were both schizophrenic, there's a good chance that you are too. Right?"

Her voice rose. "Who cares about your childhood? Who cares if you were beaten and abused as a child?"

Sara jerked up and poked her index finger into my chest. "Does anybody care if your Daddy loves you?"

"It's none of your business."

Sara grinned. "Fair enough. But psychiatrists cure mentally ill patients with drugs every day. They spend years in training to recognize different illnesses. Then they spend more years learning how to treat them.

Psychologists think they treat people by talking to them. Some of their patients get better on their own.

The rest of them realize it is a waste of time. They either stop going or kill themselves. They think they will never improve. The smart ones see a psychiatrist, and get better."

I wanted to ask Sara if she cured anyone during her psychiatric rotation, until I heard her take a deep breath.

"I hope the person who decided psychologists are Doctors collapses in their office! And I hope they send that patient to me."

It made perfect sense to me. Too bad for them. Sara understood everything that I didn't know. I grabbed her neck and pulled her lips next to mine. I forgot my germophobia and stuck my tongue in her mouth for a second.

Sara shoved me away. She wiped her mouth with a tissue. My brain was searching for a suitable response, when Sara started her car. "Put on your seat belt. I'm taking you home."

Sara lurched out of her parking space on Warren Street. She made an illegal u–turn, to make an illegal right turn, to drive Uptown on West Street.

New York City condemned the West Side Highway in 1973. West Street replaced the elevated West Side Highway below 57th Street.

Sara raced taxis up West Street. I pondered the value of a reduced life expectancy against Sara's excitement. The half–pint in my pocket bounced against my chest, as Sara screeched to a stop at a red light.

I opened the bottle and offered it to Sara. She accepted it, took a sip and returned it. "I'm sorry. I wasn't trying to scare you. I'm a pilot. Pilots like to drive fast."

I finished the bottle while I pictured a naked Sara turning off her plane's engines. We glided through space, until she climaxed or we crashed.

My nightmare ended when Sara pulled over to the curb. "I'll stop at a liquor store near my house. You never asked, but I live on 102nd Street off Riverside. Please get rid of the bottle. I don't drive with empty bottles in my car."

There was no litter basket, so I flung the bottle 400 feet onto the empty West Side Highway. We waited for its crash.

Sara patted the top of my head. She bellowed, "Good shot!"

Sara swerved around a homeless person pushing a shopping cart. How many vagrants began their descent after a psychologist's treatment? I bought two quarts at the liquor store.

We entered her one bedroom apartment on the first floor of a brownstone. A spinet piano and convertible couch filled the living room. Her open bedroom door revealed a mattress and alarm clock on a bare wooden floor.

She kicked off her shoes and sat on the couch. "Make me a drink and get over here."

At least she liked to drink. I filled two water glasses with whiskey and brought them to the couch.

Sara took a sip. "Take off your shoes. I don't like shoes in the house."

I finished half of my drink before I sat down and looked around her living room.

I asked, "Do you have a TV?"

Sara replied, "I don't need a TV. I have you."

Over the weekend we decided to get married and breed two children. On Sunday, we filled the back seat of her car with the contents of my hotel room.

I became accustomed to Sara's bellowing and orders. We were married in the Municipal Building, six days after we met. Our first married activity was a walk to Mickey's Bar.

Mickey's was closed. A large sign on its window said it would reopen in a month as a gay health club.

Sara and I were the last married couple to meet at Mickey's Bar. We belonged together.

Mankind, Womankind, Kidkind

"Come on, Sara. You've never been to Brooklyn?"

"I almost went once. The guy before you was arrested in Brooklyn, for jumping a subway turnstile. He wanted me to take a cab there, to bail him out. He's the ex–boyfriend because I know you would never do that."

"Of course not, Darling."

Sara searched my eyes for truth. "I never had any reason to go there. Do you want to show me where you grew up?"

"Let's go tomorrow. We can take the subway to Sheepshead Bay to visit my parents. They are living in the same apartment for 31 years. Let's stop at Chris's Bar on the way back. It's my favorite place to drink, and they serve decent food. Whenever we get there, we will meet someone who went to high school with me."

"I owe you one for spending a day at my sister's house last week. Her useless husband left us alone all day."

"I never met anyone as useless as him in my whole life. Why is your sister married to him for almost twenty years?"

"She's not smart. She thinks they have to stay together for their kids."

Sara yawned and turned off her reading lamp. "I will do whatever you want, as long as you never get stupid or useless. If you expect me to be in a good mood tomorrow, you better not be useless now."

We decided six weeks was a respectable dating period. We had two weeks to go before we could surprise everyone with our marriage.

There are always a couple of details to work out before a marriage.

Sara wanted us to have hyphenated last names so she could keep using her medical, driver's and pilot's licenses. She also wanted me to get a "real" job, but I loved my job.

I was a "Lock Box Product Specialist" at a Midtown bank. My pay was okay. The benefits were great. I was important enough to hold keys to the executive bathroom and dining room. I wrote short stories while I waited for a telephone to ring, or an interoffice envelope delivery.

Sara visited me at work.

She enjoyed the panoramic views from the rooftop dining room on the 54th floor. She sat on the visitor's chair in my cubicle after lunch, and read my stories until five o'clock.

Sara liked my stories. But she disliked my job. My phone did not ring, and nobody delivered interoffice mail to me all afternoon.

I wanted to sit in my cubicle until I received a Fossil watch and a monthly pension check for two decades of service.

Outside the building, Sara said, "You have two weeks to get a real job. I don't care what they're paying you to sit there. My husband has to do something useful."

Sara had two real jobs. She was in the second year of a three year surgical residency program at St. Donna's Hospital. Sara moonlighted in an emergency room on Long Island, for one weekly twelve hour shift.

Sara preferred working nights for car accidents, stabbings and shootings.

Sara could save your life.

Sunny Summer Sundays are rare in New York City.

Millions of city residents expect to enjoy Sunday at the beach. My parents lived ten blocks from Manhattan Beach. But visiting a New York City beach was a special event for most residents, especially the poorer ones.

Families packed as much food, drinks, umbrellas and toys, as they could carry on and off a train. Teenagers brought giant "boom boxes."

Sara and I changed trains at Columbus Circle. We waited at the downtown end of the platform and were fortunate to get seats in the first car. We sat across from a family with two young boys, and a baby.

The mother needed a nap. When she finally got settled for an hour ride, her baby started to cry.

Her husband ignored them. He opened a newspaper and distributed comics. The boys argued about the comics, while Mom fed their baby brother.

Mom held her baby with one hand while she delivered a slap to the cheek of her nearest child. "The next time I do that we're going home. Do you both understand?"

Her husband opened a can of beer. He placed it in a paper bag and muttered, "You know what will happen after we get home."

"Why do they do this?" said Sara.

"Imagine if you lived in a small apartment, or didn't have air conditioning. They bring enough stuff to stay at the beach as long as possible."

We arrived at the Sheepshead Bay station an hour later.

I used a public telephone to notify my parents. Mother hated surprise visits. She was an unmedicated schizophrenic, because Dad liked her that way.

Dad waited for us downstairs.

Dad was thin, 5'6" tall. He seemed shorter because he leaned forward from back problems. He was bald with short gray hair on the sides of his head, and bright blue eyes. His constant amusement was evident from deep laugh lines, framing a smile.

My father grew up in a poor family where seven children shared three beds. Three brothers considered World War II an opportunity to get their own beds.

Only two brothers could serve our nation at the same time. Uncle Jerry, an aspiring violinist, stayed home to protect his delicate hands.

Dad completed twenty–seven missions as a tail gunner on a B–17. He left part of his mind in Europe.

Dad only wore his false teeth for meals and work. He greeted family and friends by sucking their cheek between his gums and licking it.

"Hello to you, my wonderful son. And you must be his wonderful girlfriend."

I closed my eyes and waited, but Sara screeched.

"What are you doing? You don't even know me."

Dad licked me before answering Sara. "You're right. I'll wait until the next time you come here."

Dad waited for Sara to wipe her cheek with a tissue. "My wife is not feeling well today. She does not want any visitors. Please call her a week in advance, if you want to come here again."

The last time I recalled my mother having a good day was on her birthday in 1966. We watched TV and ate birthday cake while we waited for Grandpa to call from Miami Beach, after the rates went down at 5 P.M.

Mother's happiness ended when Grandpa's second wife Linda called at 4:30. Linda said Grandpa was never calling again, and "by the way, he made a new will."

Sara and I left without going upstairs.

"I hate spit," she said. "I can't stand spit. Do you know what's in it?"

"What about my spit?"

Sara shrugged. "Your spit's okay. Keep him away from me. I didn't think anyone could have a crazier family than me. Our crazy families will affect our kids."

We walked across the Ocean Avenue foot bridge to Manhattan Beach. The Esplanade led us to Mrs. Stahl's Restaurant, for mushroom knishes and espresso sodas.

Sara liked Mrs. Stahl's knishes. I broke into Brooklynese. "What's not to like?"

My only concern was cash. Before I met Sara I always carried $50 loose in my pocket. She complained and got me to start carrying a wallet, a credit card and one of the new ATM cards from Citibank.

"I forgot the wallet. I only have ten dollars. Do you have any cash?"

"Why should I have cash? You wanted to come here."

"Let's have a drink at Chris's Bar. I haven't been there in two months."

"You better hope I like it, or it's going to be a lot longer than two months next time."

We got off the train at Avenue M and walked six blocks to Chris's Bar.

Sara was surprised because most of the stores were open and busy on Sunday. I explained, "This is a Jewish neighborhood. These stores are closed on Saturdays."

I don't understand what attracts people to certain places, but I loved going to Chris's Bar. It was a club. I pointed across the street while we waited for the traffic light at Coney Island Avenue. "There it is."

"You expect me to go there? It doesn't even have a sign."

"Sure it does. I'll show you."

The sign was a license to sell liquor, taped to the lower right corner of the front window.

"See? It's 'Avenue M Tavern'. There's the sign. The only time you see the name is on the calendars Chris gives out for Christmas."

Chris was the ideal saloon keeper. He didn't drink or associate with women. He owned the bar's corner building and an eight–room rooming house next door.

Chris lived in one room of his rooming house, where female visitors were not allowed. He kept one room vacant for customers who were hiding from loan sharks, bookies or wives.

Chris's main interest was betting on horses. He went to Aqueduct or Belmont almost every day on the express bus that stopped in front of his bar.

Chris refused to install a juke box to keep the bar full of dependable male drinkers. He thought a juke box would attract women and drugs.

Policemen like to drink, but they did not drink at Avenue M Tavern. Chris did not like policemen who might interfere with his bar's business.

If a customer had anything to do with law enforcement, Chris warned the regulars to stay away from him. Unlike everyone else, police never received drinks on the house.

I showed a calendar to Sara after our eyes adjusted to the near–darkness. It was helpfully posted on the inside wall. "See? It says, 'Where Good Fellows Meet'. This is a good place, full of good fellows."

The calendar did not impress Sara. "Get me a Scotch," she said. "Don't tell anyone that I am a Doctor."

It was five minutes after noon, Sunday opening time. Three people sat at the long wooden bar.

Michael Ryan and his charming wife Joan, sat in the front of the bar, with their backs to the front window. Mike was a retired fireman, and the weekday bartender.

He held his first shot of Winslow for the day. He examined it in a narrow shaft of sunlight before he bellowed, "Nectar of the Gods!" Mike followed his shot with a sip of beer and a puff on an unfiltered cigarette.

Joan was prim and proper. I never saw her in shorts or even short sleeves. She turned to me. "Top of the morning! And you, with such a lovely lady. Will you please introduce us?"

Sara did not care much for foreigners except the Irish. She had a subscription to an Irish theater company and loved their accents. Joan's accent was real.

Joan was not beautiful. She was kind, caring, attentive. Short, slim, flat–chested, with a round haircut. Her bright red hair clashed with bright yellow teeth when she smiled.

I must have taken too long to answer. Joan patted the seat next to her. "Sit with me, Sara. Let's watch our men drink."

Louie, the weekend bartender, emerged from the bathroom in a cloud of smoke. Louie and I went to high school together.

"Hi Louie. I guess Chris is gone today." Chris did not like people smoking marijuana in the bathroom unless there was a storm outside.

Customers generally sat on the front steps of his rooming house to smoke. Chris wasn't against anything that would keep customers in his bar. He didn't like the smell.

If someone wanted to smoke marijuana they said, "I'm going outside to check the air pressure." The bartender preserved their seat, drink and change.

"I've got killer weed," said Louie. He handed me a joint. "Take the babe out."

"Hey Louie! The babe wants a Scotch on the rocks. I'll have a Winslow on the rocks."

Louie giggled. "I forgot I was working."

I toasted Mike and Joan. I had $7, but Sara needed drinks. She was laughing with Joan about something. A voice on my right said, "So you moved to Manhattan and now you're too good to say 'Hello' to your old friends?"

I recognized Don's voice. He enjoyed saying, "I used to work for the Post Office, now I work here. I like this better."

Joan and Don were the same size. Don was 70, always well dressed, in clean dress pants and a shirt from Sears. He had a thick Lower East Side accent and sunken cheeks from sucking on cigarettes.

"Hi Don."

"Are you going to introduce me? Or do I have to buy her drinks until she thinks I am you?"

Sara turned away from Joan and smiled at Don. "I'm Sara. I would love to have a drink with you. This cheapskate, who claims he loves me, brought me to a bar with ten dollars."

Louie interrupted everyone. "Anyone else want a hamburger? I'm starving."

Sara pouted until I said, "I will buy one for this beautiful lady."

Don waved at Louie. "I'll buy her a drink. Her boyfriend is a cheapskate."

Louie wiped his hands and carried a fresh glass to Sara. He winked at me and said, "My girlfriend Doris will be here soon. She knows lots of rich guys. Want me to call her, ask her to bring one for you?"

Three boys in their early twenties diverted our attention. They might have been brothers. They were all wearing jeans, white t–shirts and Yankee caps. The boys looked at the blank TV before the oldest one asked, "Are youse gonna watch the Yankee game?"

Louie pointed to the big TV in front. "Sorry. It's not working today."

Another boy pointed to the smaller TV in the rear. "What about that one?"

"That TV hasn't worked in years."

The three huddled until the oldest asked, "Can we get a six–pack of Schaefer to go?"

"Sorry," said Louie. "We don't sell beer to go. Try the bar on Avenue O." The boys left and walked towards Avenue O.

"The TV is broken? We don't sell beer to go?" said Mike.

Louie wrote "Out of order" on a piece of paper and taped it to the TV screen.

"Did you want them here? They would make noise, spill beer and not tip me. If you wanted to sell them a six–pack, you should have done it yourself. This way they won't come back," said Louie.

Mike sighed and raised his hands in disgust. "What is wrong with the younger generation? When I work, I am here to serve mankind, womankind and kidkind! I give everybody a drink."

He noticed Joan's disapproving look and added, "I only give kids drinks when their parents are here."

"That's better," said Joan.

"Hey Louie! You better buy us this round or I'm telling Chris you refused to serve three customers," said Mike.

Louie shrugged. "I'll buy everybody a drink."

Other bars put poker chips in front of you when you had a drink coming. Chris's Bar gave you another drink.

Sara had three drinks in front of her. She raised one glass to me. "I can see why you come here."

"Wait. You haven't seen the best part. We're going to check the air pressure."

"Go. Leave an old man alone with his fantasies. I'll watch your drinks," said Don.

"Come on, Sara. You will like this."

We walked out of Chris's back door into harsh sunlight. I held Sara's hand and led her down Avenue M, to the next block. We made a left turn on East Tenth Street. I pulled out Louie's joint on the side street.

"Surprise!" Sara usually loved surprises.

I lit the joint, turned it backwards in my mouth and turned to kiss her. Before she realized it, I was blowing a stream of smoke into her mouth.

Sara coughed. "What are you doing? I can't do anything illegal out in the street. I could lose my malpractice insurance."

"I know you like to smoke pot after drinks. Don't worry about your insurance. You are in Brooklyn, no one cares. The police are busy, looking for murderers and kidnappers."

I made my point when a speeding police car passed us.

Sara shrugged. We finished smoking.

Inside, Sara pointed to the Joker Poker machine. "Does that really pay off?"

"Of course. You need at least forty credits, ten dollars, to cash in. There's another one in the Swan Bar, on Church Avenue. The Swan Bar's machine pays cash, like Atlantic City."

"Isn't that illegal?"

When I did not reply, Sara said, "I forgot. The cops are too busy chasing real criminals."

Fred was walking in the front door when we returned to our seats. I went to high school with Fred. Everyone called Fred "Living Legend" or "Double–Ell." But nobody, including Fred, could remember why.

Fred sat next to Don. He ordered a draft beer. "Hey Louie! What happened to the TV? I bet on the Yankees."

"Would you mind listening to the game on the radio?"

"No. I can check the score later."

I led Sara over to Fred. "This is Fred, the Living Legend. Hey Fred, this is Sara. She won't marry me until I quit my wonderful job. Please tell her about your job."

Fred showed Sara his biggest smile. "I work for a bank."

Sara sighed. "So does he."

Fred nodded. "I'm a computer operator on the third shift.

I do all my work in fifteen minutes. I load the paper and start a reporting program. Then I set an alarm for four hours and go to sleep.

I have to get up once to make sure the paper didn't jam. I sleep another three hours, unload the paper and go home.

I can retire in nine years, and meet Don here in the morning."

Fred raised his glass. "Here's to working at Chris's!"

He put down his empty glass. Fred removed a full set of false teeth, wrapped them in a napkin and placed them in his shirt pocket. Fred saw Sara watching him. "I don't need them. I already ate."

Sara placed her arm on my shoulder and whispered, "I don't care if he's your friend. Promise me that you'll kill him if he tries to kiss me."

"I'm down to my last dollar. He won't have a chance today."

"Give me that dollar."

Sara walked to the Joker Poker machine. Don crooned "Whatever Lola Wants," before slipping me a twenty dollar bill. Don sounded like a professional singer, despite years of heavy smoking. He liked to entertain us with the first line of Broadway songs.

"Thanks Don." I waved to Doris as she entered, on my way to join Sara.

Sara had been reading the instructions. She pressed "Deal" as I arrived. Sara pulled a Royal Flush and won $100.

She did not seem surprised. "See what happens when you listen to me? You better do whatever I want!"

"What should I do?"

"Get me more pot. But you can't bring any home."

A cheer erupted from the bar. Louie was kissing Doris while he raised her petite body over the bar and placed her beside him.

Sara waited for them to break their embrace before bellowing, "Hey Louie! Get over here. I've got a Royal Flush. You owe me a hundred dollars. Take out enough to buy everybody a drink."

Mike bellowed, "Hurray for mankind, womankind and kidkind with parents!"

Sara bellowed back, "You better give everyone a double!"

Nobody gave orders better than Sara.

Christmas Surprises

Christmas is one of the most confusing topics for Jews.

Some Christians spend months preparing for it. I always tried to feign enthusiasm in their presence. I hoped Sara was not one of them, when I introduced the subject. Sara said Christmas was just another day.

She suggested a drive to Long Island, because traffic would be lighter. Sara loved driving her new car, a maroon Dodge Charger with a stick shift.

I brought $400 cash, hoping for a Christmas surprise.

Sara steered with three fingers, while she discussed current events. She said her "Police Surgeon" card would prevent her from receiving a speeding ticket.

Sara loved surprises.

I surprised her for the first time, two weeks after we met. Sara said she would meet me downtown, after her dentist appointment on West 58th Street. I was ready a couple of hours early and wanted to surprise her.

We posed for photos the day before, in a booth at the Midtown Arcade on Broadway and 49th Street. I had her photo in my wallet when I took the subway to Columbus Circle.

I showed her photo to five doormen before I found her. Sara was in a building with a Central Park South address. But there was an entrance for the professional apartments on West 58th Street.

Sara giggled when I entered the waiting room.

Now it was her turn.

We entered a small airport. Sara parked next to a storefront with "Eon Air" painted on its front window.

A gray metal desk and three wooden chairs from the 1920's filled Eon Air's office. A dozen folded metal chairs rested against one wall, but there was no room to open them.

Marty, the owner and sole employee, sat behind the desk in the largest chair. Marty was hunched over a ledger, writing with his face next to the page. There were two overflowing ashtrays on his desk.

Marty was about 70, five feet tall, with a full head of uncombed white hair. He wore a dark green flight suit. Two large magnifying lenses in a black plastic frame, covered his eyes.

Marty looked up when he finished writing. "Oh Sara, it's you."

Sara signed some forms. Marty handed her others for her pre–flight check. She had about thirty things to check. I watched and tried to follow. Being with Sara was a perpetual learning experience.

Marty was hunched over the same book when we returned to his office. This time he looked up immediately. Sara handed him a clipboard. Marty glanced at the forms. "Please try to be back by five."

Sara rented a Cessna 152: one propeller, two seats, almost no cargo space.

We strapped in, and like everything else in her charmed life, Sara made flying look easy. We were going to Martha's Vineyard. Sara had never been there. She chose places with small airports. Sara avoided the routes used by large, commercial jets.

Sara handed me a map after takeoff. She explained how she navigated with maps, not instruments.

Sara's "IFR" was "I Follow Roads." We followed roads and approached Martha's Vineyard an hour later. Sara received landing and parking instructions on the radio.

We left the plane and walked toward a line of three taxis. It was a sunny day, in the 40's. The drivers were chatting outside.

"Can one of you fellows please take us somewhere nice for lunch?" I said.

The drivers thought they heard the funniest joke of all–time.

One driver stopped laughing to say, "You can't eat anywhere on Christmas without a reservation."

I held up three twenties. "Here's $60 to take us to eat. $20 for the ride and $40 more if we get in."

The drivers huddled before one fellow pointed to his cab. "I know a place you can try."

We traveled for ten minutes on narrow roads. We passed invisible houses, hidden behind gates and winding driveways. The driver finally turned onto a narrower street, partially blocked by limousines. He parked on the sidewalk. We were 100 feet away from the restaurant where I intended to eat lunch as soon as possible.

I told the cab driver to come inside to collect his $40 if I did not return in an hour. Otherwise, I would return sooner and give him $20 for a ride back to the airport. He said, "Good luck," and opened a newspaper.

Back in my college days, I worked Summers at Grossinger's Hotel in the Catskills – first as a busboy, later as a waiter.

You can see Richard Dreyfuss at my old job in his first movie, *The Apprenticeship of Duddy Kravitz*. It was hectic, barely controlled chaos. Some ravenous Jews ordered five portions of lox for breakfast.

Christian chaos was subdued. A black velvet curtain separated the dining room and bar. A velvet rope, protected by an officious fellow wearing a Santa–red satin jacket, blocked the public. He stood behind a lectern that held a large reservation book and a small telephone.

I wanted to tell him what happened at the airport because he looked like he had not laughed in years. He gave me directions to the men's room.

Sara got a cappuccino, though not a seat, at the bar. I stood near the bathroom, and acted like I was waiting for someone.

I stopped a busboy and handed him $20. "Please tell your waiter I have more money for both of you. Ask him to speak to me. I will wait here."

I gave the waiter $60 and another $40 to the busboy. The waiter told me to stand there and wait. They returned a moment later, carrying a small table, tablecloth and two chairs.

They miraculously setup this table in the middle of an aisle, where there did not appear to be any space. It nearly touched two other tables.

The busboy called me over. He opened the other side of the curtain so I could get Sara's attention and lead her in. Sara's surprised expression made it all worthwhile, as I waited at her private entrance to this inner sanctum.

The waiting room crowd was glum. Drunks at the bar had limo drivers, everyone else wished they could be drinking. Sara was at the curtain, when one of those drunks, wearing a suit that cost more than I made in a month, grabbed her sleeve.

Sara jerked it away and continued walking to our table, where our waiter was graciously waiting to seat her. The drunk pushed past the busboy and tried to grab her. My peripheral vision registered a flash of red. Our humorless host protected Sara's seat. The drunk pointed to Sara. "She does not belong here. I am an attorney and I will…"

Our host held up his hand. "Sir, you are drunk. I will have you removed from the premises if you say another word. Please come with me."

Sara and I were seated as they left. Diners at nearby tables asked their dining companions if they recognized us.

We were in Marty's office three hours later, waiting for him to stop writing.

"Oh Sara, it's you," said Marty, before he signed her log book.

Sara and I drove back to Manhattan to make love and exult in our togetherness.

Amelia Meets Grandpa

Sara was sitting on our living room couch, balancing a rocks glass on her knee when I got home from work.

"I'll be right there, Darling." I put my sports jacket and tie on our bedroom door knob, got a drink and sat next to her. I should have kissed her, before I got a drink. Sara responded well to my late kiss. The last time I got a drink before I kissed her she said, "I know what your priorities are now."

"I can tell you've had a bad day," said Sara. "Tell me about it. Then I'll tell you about my day."

"I wanted to quit. I don't feel like discussing it. How was your day?"

Sara finished her drink and laughed.

"It's a good thing you didn't quit. I quit. One of us needs a job."

"What happened?"

Sara got up to refill her glass.

"Louise quit. She's moving back to Michigan to stay with her mother."

Louise was Sara's Chief Resident. We went to Louise's small apartment every couple of weeks for sushi.

Sara loved "talking shop." Surgeons love cutting anything complicated with sharp knives.

Louise combined their interests with sushi in her Barrow Street apartment. Sherry, a pediatric orthopedist from St. Donna's, often joined us.

Two or three large fish packed in ice filled Louise's kitchen counter. A rice cooker, sushi knives, a diamond–encrusted knife sharpener and a variety of seasonings were on an adjacent table.

The ladies cut fish while I watched cable TV on Louise's delightful water bed. Sara brought me concoctions to try, until I fell asleep.

"Louise loved surgery," I said.

"Not any more. She cut herself yesterday and tested positive for hepatitis. What am I supposed to do? Wear two pairs of gloves? I want healthy children. I'm going to do something else. Maybe psychiatry.

I lined up a job with an agency, working nights in an E.R. for forty dollars an hour. I'll be able to afford a course to get my instrument rating. We will be able to rent nicer planes. It's a small E.R. You can visit me on weekends."

Patients were lucky if Sara was working. An ambulance arrived while we chatted in her lounge, on my last visit to this Emergency Room job.

Two EMTs brought in a tall fellow wearing a white linen suit. His face was blue, a wet stain messed up his pleated pants. A nurse coming to work, was chatting with an EMT. Sara said, "Get dressed, Judy. And please dress my husband."

Sara's tall patient was breathing when Judy and I arrived at his stretcher. He regained consciousness, and tried to remove his oxygen mask. Sara pushed his hands down. She delivered the usual speech about being in a hospital. I was dying to tell him he was lucky to be alive.

He pushed Sara away, sat up and removed his oxygen mask. He said, "I am a lawyer and I demand…"

We never heard his demand because Sara injected something into a tube that sent him to la–la–land.

Sara checked his vital signs before filling up a page of his chart with a comment. She added a Post-It note to the top sheet, and dropped the chart in its aluminum pocket on the front of the stretcher.

"That's it for him," she said.

Sara walked around the stretcher. She unlocked the wheels and watched her patient sleep for a moment. Sara suddenly shoved the stretcher across the room. It crashed into unused stretchers.

Sara pointed to Judy. "Leave him for the next shift."

Judy froze. Sara walked over to Judy until their noses were an inch apart. "I suppose you want to ask me something. What do you want? Get it over with."

Judy bawled like a baby.

Sara stepped back to avoid Judy's tears. I hoped Sara never looked at me the way she was glaring at Judy.

The smack of Sara's right palm on Judy's left cheek filled the room.

"Pull yourself together, or go home! It's bad enough that I have to treat lawyers. Do you understand?"

Judy whispered, "May I please move that stretcher?"

Sara giggled. "That's a good idea. Put the lawyer in number two, behind a curtain. I don't want to see him. Check him every fifteen minutes. Let me know if he starts to wake up."

I reached for Sara's hand, to lead her back to the lounge for coffee. She pulled away from me. Her eyes turned black while her face contorted into a hideous grin.

Sara bent her neck back until her mouth faced the ceiling. "I hate lawyers! Does everyone understand? I hate lawyers!"

I don't know what everyone was doing before her bellow, but they all stopped. It was eerie being in a quiet emergency room, with a couple of beeping monitors. Employees I had never seen gathered by the nurse's station. I relaxed when the automatic doors opened for Larry, Sara's supervisor and relief. Sara ignored him. "Am I the only person who is working in this hospital?"

The crowd dispersed and the noise returned. Larry was grinning. "Rough night, Sara?"

"Call psych and transfer number two. Everything is in his chart. Find someone to replace me. I quit."

Sara took my hand and led me to her car without changing out of her greens. She was quiet until we left the hospital parking lot.

"We need a drink. I'll pull outside a store. You can run in. You're too serious. You're more fun after you've had a few drinks."

We opened our half–pint bottles after she found a legal parking spot. Sara clinked my bottle, took a big slug and chuckled.

"The record says I had to keep him sedated because he was suicidal. Did you hear him threaten to kill himself?"

"I only heard him threaten to sue you."

"Maybe I misunderstood him. No harm, no foul. Three days in a bin will be good for him. I left Harris a note. He's working psych. Harris was sued twice this year. I hope he sends the lawyer to Bellevue, and forgets to notify his family."

We finished our drinks. I disposed of the bottles in a litter basket.

Sara was quiet until we got upstairs.

"I never want to work with anyone like Judy again. She should get a job making coffee and forget about being a nurse. O.R. nurses are much better. They take orders.

I want to get back into an operating room. I can't do anything about it today. Let's talk about something else. I want to meet your parents. Your mother, anyway."

"I would like to meet your parents too."

Sara visited my parents first. Mother made her specialty, roast beef topped with canned stewed tomatoes. I learned about her secret ingredients, sugar and MSG, years later. Mother served canned peaches topped with frozen raspberries in syrup for dessert.

Unfortunately, an uninvited guest interrupted our meal. I looked up from my roast beef and saw a dark gray mouse licking up sauce from the kitchen floor. Mother was not the greatest housekeeper. She cleaned the bathroom before a visitor arrived. "Otherwise people will think we live like pigs."

I yelled, "A mouse!" and stamped my feet. Dad muttered, "Ignore it and it will go away."

"What an embarrassment, in front of my new daughter–in–law. She'll think we live like pigs," said Mother.

Sara whispered, "Stop. You'll scare it. I need an empty mayo jar, peanut butter and a piece of cardboard."

Sara spooned peanut butter on the card and ordered us to be quiet. She stood two feet from her bait and waited.

After a flash of sudden movement, Sara held a trapped mouse in the jar. "Take me to the incinerator," she said.

Mother whispered, "Nobody has to know about this. They'll think we live like pigs."

During the drive back to our Upper West Side apartment, I told Sara it was time for me to visit her parents. They lived in rural Ohio. Sara was afraid of her father, Bob.

After an early bed–wetting period, Bob tied her to the tree in their front yard with her wet sheet.

As a teen, Sara's punishments began when Bob handed her the folding knife he wore on his belt and said, "Cut me a switch."

Her big brother Ted, a Vietnam veteran, ended the beatings. Ted restrained Bob and explained how he would kill him and bury him in the woods, if he ever touched Sara again. Ted lived across the road from his parents. He said, "Dad became my enemy. I never spoke to him again."

Sara would not budge. Her mother was welcome to visit her. Otherwise she wanted us to visit her mother after Bob died.

I said, "Call your mother. We are visiting her this weekend and staying one night."

Sara looked downcast, but picked up the phone. I walked into the kitchen and returned when I heard her hang up. Sara's summary was, "Mom wanted to know what you liked to eat."

Sara discussed her parents during our eleven hour drive. Mom was a retired elementary school teacher. Bob failed at dairy farming. He drove a school bus for twenty–five years, retiring with a small pension. Bob's primary activity was sitting in an overstuffed leather chair with his feet up on a hassock.

He read the weekly newspaper or watched television until his wife served meals. Mom solved crosswords or played Scrabble against herself. She went to Church alone on Sundays.

We found Bob sitting near the hot fireplace, reading the weekly newspaper. He did not greet us.

Mom was delighted to see Sara for ten seconds, until Bob got our attention by snapping his newspaper.

He held it vertically, folded in thirds, and sharply pulled the outside parts in opposite directions. It was impossible to ignore.

"Dad wants to read his newspaper. Let's go outside. I want you to meet our puppy, Rocky."

Rocky was a mixed breed, a foot long, with short black hair. His feet and nose were white. Rocky lived in a green vinyl dog house, filled with blankets. Sara removed Rocky's chain.

Despite the subfreezing weather, Rocky barked at us to throw him a ball or give him a treat. Sara's mother was terror–stricken when Rocky barked. He stopped when she petted him.

I asked for directions to get Rocky a treat, and raced to the house. As expected, Rocky followed me inside. Sara and her mother followed Rocky. Mom grabbed a treat from the box, and used it to lead Rocky outside. She said, "He can't get used to being in the house."

Bob was still behind his newspaper, but something seemed different about him.

I said, "Excuse me. I married your daughter. I would like to meet you."

He swung his feet off the hassock and nudged it in my direction. I got a new view when I sat on it. A double barreled shotgun, with its hammers pulled back, was leaning against the wall, between his chair and a lamp.

Bob sat up until he was looking down at me. "I understand you want to marry my daughter, and you're a Jew. Is that right?"

Sara interrupted us. "Sonny, get your coat. Dad, how can you talk to him like that? And how can you ignore me? You haven't seen me for five years. Don't expect to see me for another five."

Sara faced her mother. "Why don't you leave him right now? Come with us."

Mom did not respond.

Ted drove her mother to Manhattan after our daughter Amelia was born. They slept in adjoining rooms at the Belleclaire Hotel on 77th Street for two nights.

Amelia enjoyed playing with her new relatives. There were no arguments. During goodbyes her mother said, "Dad's changed. He's nicer. Why don't you bring Amelia over for a weekend, so he can meet her?"

A week later, after Amelia's first flight, we rented a car and returned to the depressing domicile. Mom came out to greet us. I don't know why, but my first question was, "Where's Rocky?"

"Dad shot him. He made too much noise," said Mom.

"Stay here," said Sara. She entered the house.

"What is wrong with you? How could you shoot that dog? Do you think I would bring a baby near you?"

Sara stormed out. "Get in the car. We're leaving. I took your advice and visited him. Don't ever mention him again."

Nobody gave orders better than Sara.

Let's Take a Bus

Sara joined the anesthesiology residency program at St. Irene's Hospital. She said she was a "scuttdog." It was her first year of a three year program.

I used my knowledge of C programming to get a job with Medical Insurance Services, on East 44th Street. Our individual $28,000 salaries covered our expenses.

MIS sold Billex, a medical practice management system for PC–compatible computers. Billex was popular in a niche, because it was one of the first products to provide electronic claims submissions to physicians.

MIS hired me as an assistant. My first jobs were changing light bulbs and proofreading instruction manuals. They trained me to answer "incident reports," after my first month. I was in charge of the "Patient Daily Visit" module, working with eight other programmers.

Sara slept at St. Irene's one weekend a month, "on call." On other Fridays, she arrived at my office about 3 PM. Sara received a warm greeting from Roger, the project manager. MIS only sold one system to an anesthesiologist. Sara and Roger discussed modifications for MIS to increase sales.

Her joke, was that Roger should remove "Patient Daily Visit," because 99% of anesthesiologists have no office visits.

Sara never worked for free. Her deal with Roger, was that I could leave early, when he got tired of listening to her complain about his product.

Sara and I walked to Grand Central Station after work on a Friday, for two dozen raw clams and oysters at The Oyster Bar. I liked Cherrystone clams, Sara preferred Bluepoint oysters. Sara swallowed hers with Scotch.

Whatever they say about shellfish is true. They are aphrodisiacs when you're eating them with your wonderful wife, who got you out of work an hour early.

Our carefree days ended, when our daughter Amelia was born two years earlier.

Amelia was the most beautiful, intelligent, well–behaved two–year–old on Earth. She never heard of "the terrible twos." In spite of that, Amelia was like adding saltpeter to my clams.

Amelia waited for us at "Our Blossoming Years," on West 104th Street. They charged parents an arm and a leg to watch their little darlings until 6 PM. After six they traded your child for a cash ransom of at least $50.

Sara touched my hand. "Let's go home." I preferred not to think of it as an order. An order might affect my virility. We got up together and walked down a ramp to the subway.

I never imagined meeting someone like Sara. I wanted to have "adult time" with her in twenty minutes, before we picked up Amelia.

My brains returned when we turned a corner. Over a hundred people were waiting outside the turnstiles.

A Transit Authority employee wearing a fluorescent orange vest stood on a ladder. He spoke through a battery–powered bullhorn.

"Due to a water main break on 44th Street and Broadway, Uptown IRT Seventh Avenue lines are out of service. The Transit Authority expects all service to be restored by 9 PM. Please standby for more information."

I turned to Sara. "Let's take a bus."

Sara shook, in an involuntary shudder. "I'd rather walk," she said.

We went outside and walked Uptown.

I thought Sara was being smart. Overflowing buses passed crowds at bus stops.

We reached the locked door of Our Blossoming Years at 6:15. Lisa, a young woman who worked in the afternoon, opened the door. "May I help you?"

Sara pushed Lisa out of the way. She waited for me to enter and slammed the door shut.

"Bring me my child."

"Sure." Lisa picked up a form and pen, and leaned over a desk. She was about to write, when Sara pulled the pen out of her hand.

"Bring me my child now!"

I bit my inner cheek to avoid laughing.

Mrs. King, the owner, appeared at another door. "Is there a problem?"

The front doorbell freed Lisa. She lost whatever comfort she might have gained, when we heard voices of parents outside.

Sara paused until they entered, before turning to Mrs. King. "Bring me my child now. Or I will have this place closed down in an hour."

Mrs. King retreated, closing the door. Sara spoke to the parents. "Do you think you should have to pay a $50 penalty on top of their ridiculous hourly overtime fee, to get your child, because the subways are not running?

You are wonderful parents for getting here so fast. Your children deserve to be cared for by decent people. My daughter is out of here. I will take a day off work on Monday to find a friendlier place. You will too, if you want what's best for you and your children."

A fully–dressed Amelia tugged on Sara's coat. "I heard your voice. You were talking loud."

I picked up Amelia. "Mommy talks loud better than anyone."

"Mommy does everything better than anyone," said Amelia.

Lisa aged ten years when she tried to hand a ransom form to a male parent. He pushed it back, before unleashing a stream of innovative obscenities.

"Daddy? Why is everyone talking so loud today?"

"It doesn't matter. Nobody speaks loud as well as Mom."

"I knew that, silly. Dad, why are you so silly?"

At home, Sara said, "I'm sorry. I know it's an inconvenience. We have to find a new place for Amelia. I couldn't let Mrs. King get away with that. The machine is blinking, see who called. I'll give Amelia a bath before dinner."

My Dad called. He had two tickets to the Giants game for us.

Dad worked as a waiter at a coffee shop on Seventh Avenue, between 57th and 58th Streets.

One of Dad's regular customers was Tim Mara, co–owner of the Giants. Mr. Mara lived around the corner at the New York Athletic Club, best–known as the home of the Heisman Trophy. He gave Dad tickets to every home game.

Mr. Mara's seats were always on the 50–yard line, in the fifth row of the first promenade. Dad gave us some of the tickets.

Sara was the first woman I met who loved football. She understood its complex rules as well as anyone. Sara became interested in football during medical school, when Tony Dorsett was the star of the Pitt Panthers.

I said, "Why don't we leave Amelia with my parents until Monday afternoon? I can take off work on Monday. I will find a new daycare place and pick her up before rush hour. It will be easier to look at daycare centers, if I am not carrying her around.

We can have fun together on Sunday. Let's bring a bottle and hang out with the tailgaters.

You don't have to drive. We can take the bus. There's a special bus from the Port Authority for Giants games. It will drop us off at the gate."

"Why do we have to take the bus? I want to drive," said Sara.

"The bus will be lots of fun, especially if the Giants win."

Sara disregarded my logic with a wave. "I don't ride on buses," she said. "Have you ever seen me take a bus?"

I thought about it. "No. We never took a bus together. I take the number five bus home after I visit Dad. It's never crowded. It's slower than the subway, but it drops me right on Riverside Drive and 103rd Street."

"Darling, I'm glad you like buses. I don't."

Sara described her last bus ride to me, after we put Amelia to bed. Bob whipped her with a belt for vomiting on the school bus he was driving.

I ordered her to get over it this weekend. We were taking a bus for fifteen minutes.

Sara considered it for a moment, and agreed.

We went to Brooklyn on Friday, after work.

Sara and I watched *Terms of Endearment* at the Kingsway theater, on Friday night. Sara was on a Shirley MacLaine kick. She enjoyed reading MacLaine's autobiography, *Out on a Limb*.

I was not fond of Shirley MacLaine or serious movies. The last two movies I liked were *Airplane!* and *Caddyshack*. I kept quiet because marriage requires flexibility.

Amelia threw up Grandma's breakfast. Sara said Amelia vomited because she did not want us to leave her with my parents on Sunday. Whenever I questioned Sara's pronouncements, she said, "I'm a Doctor. Listen to me."

I walked to Sheepshead Bay Road to buy six half–pints for the game: Winslow for me, Scotch for Sara. I only told Sara about four bottles. We played Candyland and Clue with Amelia all day.

Sara's examination of Amelia the following morning, seemed a little too thorough. I thought she was looking for an excuse to avoid the bus. But Amelia was fine.

Sara and I put on thermal underwear, sweaters, heavy coats, gloves and knitted hats. She carried a large blanket to cover our legs. I wrapped four bottles in a scarf and stuffed them into a torn coat pocket.

I kept the other two bottles in separate pockets. Sara's coat pockets contained two roast beef sandwiches from Dad.

Sara ordered my parents to keep Amelia indoors.

We walked across the street to the Sheepshead Bay subway station, and boarded an empty, rear car. Sara finished one bottle before we reached the Manhattan Bridge.

A bus was waiting for our fifteen minute ride, to meet joyous fans in the Meadowlands parking lot. Giants won seven of their first twelve games. They only won three out of sixteen games, during the previous season. It was their second season under Bill Parcells, their greatest coach.

Fans hoped the Giants would finish with a winning record for the first time in ten years.

Giants opponents were the five and seven Kansas City Chiefs. Chiefs were on a three game losing streak.

Sara and I finished our second half–pints in the parking lot, before entering the stadium.

It was a disappointing game until the last minute and a half. Lawrence Taylor sacked Todd Blackledge. Blackledge fumbled. Harry Carson picked up the loose ball, and carried it into the end zone. Giants trailed 27–21 after the kick.

A palpable, electric surge ran through the frigid crowd, as the Giants lined up for an onside kickoff.

I pulled out my last two bottles and handed one to Sara. "Surprise!"

"Now I know why I married you," she said.

Giants recovered their own kickoff. They scored a touchdown two plays later and tied the game with one second on the clock. Sara and I finished our bottles while Ali Haji–Sheik kicked the extra point to win the game, after time expired.

Sara and I thought we saw the greatest Giants game of all–time.

"Jubilant" is not enough to describe the rest of the crowd.

Sara and I missed the first bus. We were at the front of the line for the second bus.

We sat on a two–person bench in the middle because Sara wanted to face the front. The bus was cold. Sara draped the blanket over our legs.

I got an erection thinking about sitting next to the greatest woman I ever met. I do not know if I said anything. Sara recognized it. She began unzipping my pants under the blanket as the bus started moving.

Screaming passengers exceeded the bus's legal limit. Their noise excited me. I pulled down my pants under the blanket. Sara lowered her pants and thermal underwear. In seconds, she was bouncing on my lap, bellowing, "Oh! Oh!"

I looked up to see the fellow next to me smiling. I shrugged my shoulders, closed my eyes, found Sara's rhythm. Someone clapped his hands and yelled, "Go! Go! Go!" The other passengers joined in.

Sara and I screamed in simultaneous orgasms, before we reached Manhattan. The passengers applauded.

A wise guy shouted, "More!" I closed my pants and stood up. Our fans waited for a speech. I said, "No more." Sara received a thunderous ovation after she waved to the grinning passengers.

We undressed together, after the game. Sara pointed to a piece of gum, stuck to her hip.

"That was fun. But don't ask me to ride on a bus again."

Nobody gave orders better than Sara.

Final Jeopardy!

Sara was in the second year of a three year anesthesiology residency at St. Irene's Hospital. She came home from work on a frigid day, with exciting news.

"A rich guy from Florida who manages anesthesiology practices, gave me my first job offer. He wants to give me a $50,000 interest free loan for two years, to help with our expenses.

I have to agree to work at one of his practices for at least two years after I finish my residency."

Sara poured herself a drink before she continued. "His name is Mel. He's a real character.

We're spending the weekend at the Jacksonville Beach Suites. Mel's sending cars to pick us up Friday night and take us home on Sunday. He's paying for everything. The hotel has five restaurants."

We landed in Jacksonville. Jacksonville Beach was gorgeous.

Our fifth floor hotel room faced the pool. Amelia woke us at dawn to turn on the television. I disinfected the telephone and remote control with rubbing alcohol, before ordering breakfast.

Sara emerged from the bathroom in full makeup, wearing a business suit.

Our phone rang while we are eating. I heard, "Sure Mel. See you in fifteen minutes."

Sara turned to me. "You're on your own this weekend. I brought plenty of sun block for Amelia. Please keep her covered. Use your room key to pay for everything. Get room service. Order whatever you want. I will be back tonight by ten. Mel wants me to meet lots of people."

Sara kissed Amelia. Amelia said, "Bye Mommy," before returning to her cartoon show. Cable television was a major treat for Amelia. Sara and I rarely watched television. We never ordered cable. We wanted our little angel to read books instead of watching TV. Sara thought television made children stupid.

Amelia was covered with sunblock while she played miniature golf for the first time. We were tired when she finished the course three hours later.

The Italian restaurant's superb food and air conditioning revived us. We had manicotti and spumoni. Mel bought Amelia a coloring book and crayons at the gift shop before her rest period.

"Daddy? Will we be able to live in this hotel, if Mommy gets her job?"

I sat on Amelia's bed while she opened her crayons. "People don't live in hotels forever. They live in them for a few days."

"Why do they make it so nice, if they want people to leave?"

I advised her to ask Mommy.

I started reading the USA Today and woke up two hours later. Amelia was sleeping. I woke her because I did not want her to sleep too long. We left to explore the hotel's basement.

Our first stop was the snack bar at the health club for a cup of carrot juice. Amelia enjoyed her drink, and thought Bugs Bunny would enjoy it too.

We continued our tour in the small bowling alley. They had six regular lanes. There were two lanes for duck pins: smaller pins and smaller balls. Perfect for Amelia.

Amelia was the brightest child in her age group, but rolling a ball in a straight line was not easy for her. I helped her once, before she ordered me to sit down. Amelia scored a strike 15 minutes later.

She turned around and walked to my seat. "I won. Let's go." I followed Amelia to the counter, and our room.

Amelia washed off the bowling alley. I checked for a message from Sara. Our hotel adventure continued in the Japanese restaurant.

Amelia and I were the first dinner customers.

A tall Asian woman wearing a white chef's outfit, cooked in front of us, using a large spatula and knife. She said Amelia was the most beautiful girl in the world. Our chef was certain she had seen Amelia in a movie.

In our room, Amelia asked, "Daddy? Is there someone else who looks like me?"

"Darling, I don't think anyone, except Mommy, is as beautiful as you. But there are three billion people on Earth. That's three thousand million people. It is possible that someone looks like you."

My inquisitive child was not satisfied.

"Daddy? Can we please watch a movie about a young girl on this TV? I want to make sure she does not look like me."

Our hotel television allowed us to rent almost every movie, ever made. I chose *Heidi*. Heidi is always a blonde. Amelia has dark brown hair.

We were watching *Cinderella* when Sara returned.

"How was it, Darling?"

"Tiring. Mel is a genius. He wants me to work for a straight salary, while his group collects my fees. He will guarantee $125,000 in my first year.

It sounds wonderful, but I will never see you or Amelia. I spoke to two other people who took this deal. They both work eighty hours a week."

Sara paused while she removed her pantyhose. She flung them in the general direction of our dirty laundry bag.

"The good part, is I can buy into the partnership for $75,000 after my second year. Then I would get fee–for–service. I could work normal hours and study for my boards."

Sara paused while she removed her bra.

"Anyway, the best part is Mel taught me how to skip my third year. Can you believe that?"

I held up my hand to stop her. "What do you mean?"

"There is a rule that nobody except Mel, seems to know. An anesthesiology resident can apply to be a 'hardship case.' A hardship case can skip their third year, to start making money.

Mel said Amelia is enough of a reason. I'm applying Monday. This guy is a genius. He got rich making other people rich. He thinks I should invest part of my future income in real estate with his brother, of all people."

Sara put on a night gown and got into bed. Amelia joined her while Sara continued. "He is successful. He seems honest. But he knows he is successful. I am a mere scuttdog.

He ordered me around a few times. If this is how he acts on his best behavior, what will he be like after I sign his contracts and he owns me?"

Amelia snuggled closer to Sara and pretended to be asleep.

I said, "I am going to let Mel buy me drinks."

"Please turn the light off on your way out. Use protection if you meet anyone in the night club."

"Darling, you know our deal. I will not touch a strange woman above her wrist."

Amelia opened her eyes and lifted her head. "You better not touch them above their finger."

"Okay. I won't touch anyone except you and Mommy above their finger."

Amelia said, "That's better," as I closed the door.

I followed the loudest noise in the lobby to the night club. Thelma Houston was singing "Don't Leave Me This Way." My room key got me a double Winslow at the bar. I said, "Thank you Mel," before I downed my drink and left.

I wanted to bowl a game with a full–sized ball. The elevator was full, so I walked down a staircase on the other side of the lobby. There was a "sports bar" at the bottom of these stairs. I had not noticed it when I walked around with Amelia, and it was not listed on the hotel's brochure.

The outer door closed before you opened an inner door to enter the bar. People passing in the hallway only heard noise if both doors were open.

The University of Florida Gators were playing football on eight television sets. I found a seat at the far end of the bar.

I don't recall the trip back to my room, until I met a tall woman wearing a sheer nightgown over a red negligee, and red high heels. She was about to light a cigarette when she saw me.

"My name is Opal. I'm not allowed to smoke in my room. Can you guess what color underwear I am wearing?"

It was *Final Jeopardy!* and I was about to take home the Grand Prize. Opal dropped her unlit cigarette and lighter. She opened her door and extended her arms along the door posts.

Opal carried killer germs. But I could have harmless fun with her.

I finally said, "Red."

Opal displayed surprising strength and the agility of an Olympian. She grabbed me under my armpits, before she kicked the door closed with her right high heel. I landed on top of her, on the carpeted floor of her room.

Men have two brains. We can only use one at a time. One brain said, "Be careful. She's done this before. You could catch a terrible disease."

I jumped up when I felt myself get excited.

Opal pulled her ankles toward her ears, revealing crotchless panties. She got on her knees and spread her cheeks, filling the room with a fetid odor.

I vomited on her back. I said, "Excuse me," and left her room.

Splashing cold water on my face in the lobby bathroom revived me. UCLA was playing on the basement bar's screens. Most of the crowd was gone. I was swallowing my first sip of alcohol in almost an hour, when the fellow next to me asked, "Do you follow UCLA?"

I shook my head.

"I've got no interest in watching them. This place is dead. Want to go to Cosmic Charlie's with me? It's on the other side of this road, and I have a car."

"Sure. If it's close, I can walk back later."

I finished my drink and walked with this fellow out to his car. I was so drunk that I didn't know I was drunk. He tossed me his keys. "Why don't you drive?"

He had a red Corvette convertible, and the top was down. I cannot imagine anyone turning down a chance to drive this car on a warm Winter night. Everyone I knew, except Sara and Amelia, were cold.

I said, "Where are we going?" when I started the noisy car. The passenger replied, "Over there."

He pointed to an area with bright lights, across the street. Traffic was slow. I drove through two parking lots to reach the corner. I waited for the light to change, to make two left turns.

A tall concrete median prevented me from seeing the other side of the street. Cosmic Charlie's had one small light. Most of the lights belonged to a police roadblock. I don't know why they were blocking this road. I managed to stay calm as I cruised past policemen, praying they would not stop me.

Cosmic Charlie's parking lot was full. I stopped outside the lot's entrance. I got out of the car without speaking to my passenger, and walked back to the hotel.

Opal was smoking a cigarette outside her room, wearing a black nightgown. I smiled while shaking my head. "You drank too much," said Opal. "That's all. Get over here. You're cute."

I waved "Goodbye," and unlocked my door. Amelia was in her own bed. Sara was snoring. When I got into bed I realized I forgot to brush my teeth.

Sara woke up. "Did you vomit?"

I told her the whole story.

Sara waited until I finished. "Do you realize everything bad happened after you touched Opal?"

I nodded while she sucked in a breath of air. "This is what happens when you don't listen to me." Amelia stirred in her sleep but did not wake up.

Sara had a rule: we couldn't go to sleep while either of us were angry. She turned on the TV. Unfortunately, it was tuned to CNN. News annoyed Sara. She said it proved 99% of the world is stupider than nurses.

I switched to a *Roseanne* rerun. Roseanne Barr was Sara's favorite television performer. Unlike most of TV, Sara loved her show.

We turned off the TV at the end of the show. We never mentioned this incident. I never touched another woman above the wrist.

Sara and I packed a two–cup electric pot to boil water, a single cup drip coffeemaker and coffee from Zabar's.

Sara drank two cups of Zabar's coffee before meeting Mel in the lobby at 8 AM. She said she would return for our noon checkout time. A car was meeting us at 3 PM to drive us to our 4 PM departure. Sara asked me to find something for us to do between noon and three.

I called the desk. I asked if we could please stay in our room until 2:30. The clerk was uncooperative, so I told him to charge us for another day.

Amelia and I shared waffles topped with gelatinous strawberries for lunch. Amelia consumed plenty of sugar, but it was one of our last vacation meals.

We spent almost a hundred dollars in the gift shop. Our haul included three Jacksonville Beach t–shirts. Amelia liked word search magazines, Sara liked "anything trashy." Sara's favorite newspaper was *Weekly World News*.

Our new toys kept us busy until lunch. I ordered tuna sandwiches, vanilla milk shakes and chocolate cheesecake for us. Sara's meal went into our refrigerator.

I stopped reading *The National Enquirer* when Sara arrived. Amelia stopped solving word search puzzles with her new pen. We waited for Sara to speak.

Two envelopes emerged from Sara's inside jacket pocket. "One of these is a check for $50,000. The other is a contract. I can cash the check if I sign the contract. I'm not sure if I want to do it."

I made two cups of coffee and poured Amelia a cupful of milk shake while Sara changed into a t–shirt and jeans. Sara declined my offer of a new t–shirt.

She stopped in the middle of her meal. "I forgot. It's almost one o'clock. Why are we still here?"

"Mel is paying for another day. Can he afford it?"

Sara explained how Mel made money. Hospitals knew how many operations they would perform, from their previous years of statistics.

Mel's anesthesiology group expected to bill a half million dollars for her procedures. They would pay Sara $125,000 plus $30,000 for her malpractice insurance.

Locations were San Diego and Phoenix. She thought San Diego might be nice, but it was not on her list of favorite places.

Sara covered her face and sobbed. Amelia climbed on our bed and touched her shoulder. "What's wrong, Mommy?"

Sara hugged Amelia. "I will never see my baby grow up if I take this job. I will leave before she gets up, come home after she's asleep."

Amelia patted Sara's shoulder. "It's okay Mommy. You don't have to work on this job if you don't want to."

Amelia climbed down from the bed and walked over to my chair. She put her hand on my shoulder. "Daddy, it's okay if we can't live in this hotel forever. But can we please go to the store one more time? Barbie said she's lonely without Ken."

Opal was smoking in the hallway when we left. We put down our bags. I moved Amelia's stroller out of the way before I said, "Hi Opal. This is Sara, my wife."

Sara delivered a right roundhouse punch to Opal's nose. Opal's head hit the corner of her opened door. She collapsed inside her room. Opal opened her eyes after Sara placed an ice cube tray between her legs. Sara whispered, "Stay away from my husband."

Sara was giggling in the elevator. "I haven't done that in years."

"Did you ever do that to Daddy?"

Sara smiled at a distant memory. "I never did that to Daddy. That was how I punished the cows who didn't want to come home, on my Mommy and Daddy's farm."

"Mommy, please tell me if you ever want to do that to Daddy. I want to watch you. Will you do that to Daddy if he touches a woman above her finger?"

Sara chuckled. "No, Darling. I will do something much worse."

As our elevator doors opened, Amelia said, "Did you hear that Daddy? You better not touch another woman above her fingers. Will you ever do that Daddy?"

I felt the eyes of amused onlookers, who were waiting to get in the elevator. "No."

"Good," said Amelia. She settled back in her stroller.

We stopped in the gift shop for Ken and sugarless gum. Sara said it was important for Amelia to chew gum during takeoff.

Our apartment seemed colder, darker, drearier and more crowded when we arrived at 8 PM. I picked up our mail. I showed Sara our current American Express bill. She said, "That's not so bad. We only spent $200 at Zabar's. Less than a hundred at Murray's Sturgeon Shop."

"You know what I mean. That check is tempting."

"I know what you mean."

Sara tore Mel's check in half and dropped it in the garbage.

She called Mel. "I thought it over. I would rather see my daughter grow up than work eighty hours a week."

Mel might have said "But." Sara said, "Don't you understand English?"

She hung up. "Mel offered me $200,000."

When our phone rang, I hoped it was Mel and not my parents. Sara bellowed, "Stop calling me!" She slammed down the phone.

Sara handed me a plastic grocery bag with our "Jacksonville Beach" t–shirts.

"Don't get undressed! Take these to the Salvation Army clothing drop on 96th Street right now. Get them out of here."

Nobody gave orders better than Sara.

White Saturday

Sara was approved as a hardship case. We celebrated at a new bar. Three bartenders from Mickey's, bought the Blarney Stone bar on Chambers Street.

Drinks were more expensive, until I told Ace how I met Sara.

Ace named us "The Newlyweds." He paid for our drinks and repeated our story to every customer. He wanted to put our photo behind the bar, but he couldn't find his Polaroid camera.

I took off work the following day, Sara's last day as a resident.

Her Chief wanted to meet me. Lou Peters was a past President of the American Society of Anesthesiologists. Sara described him to me on the subway.

"Lou only puts the rich and famous to sleep. He introduces himself and gives them gas. The resident gets him after the procedure.

Lou is there when the patient wakes up. I think he writes articles in his office. I only know one thing. He's going to ask me to stay."

We met Lou Peters at 9 AM. His ancient secretary Diane announced us. Lou was at his office door to greet us.

"Hi. I'm Lou Peters." His initials were on his shirt cuff, fastened by a cuff link with the Presidential seal.

We sat in two soft leather chairs and faced his movie star smile. Lou asked, "Drink?" He removed a flat silver flask of Russian vodka and three paper cups from his desk drawer.

There was a double in my cup. I was ready to ask him for a job or vote for him.

Lou raised his cup. "Here's to the smartest resident in this hospital."

"Sara's the smartest person I ever met," I said.

Sara laughed. "Stop. You're both embarrassing me."

Lou distributed three cups before he continued.

"Please don't leave. Stay another year. I'll guarantee you a fee–for–service job on staff. You'll only be on call once a month. You're brilliant. But you need more training, before you go out and kill somebody.

Something will happen that you've never seen. I'm doing this for a long time and I don't know everything.

Diane filled out your forms. You can pick them up and leave. I wish you would reconsider. Please stay another year. You can be Chief Resident and make out the schedule."

Lou finished his drink. He sprayed Binaca in his mouth while we waited for Sara to answer. I finished my drink when I heard Sara suck in a deep breath.

Sara bellowed, "Did you think a couple of drinks would make me change my mind? I'm leaving! I'm tired of being your scuttdog."

She lowered her voice. "You were a nice boss. But I've been here long enough. You live on an estate in Greenwich. I live in a one bedroom apartment. You don't remember what it's like to be poor.

I love my husband, but he doesn't make much either. Why can't you understand? It's not about you. It's about money. Don't make it personal."

Lou stood and pointed to Sara. "You're going to be a killer. A killer!"

He exhaled and sat. "You're not ready. You need another year."

I stood up. "She knows what she's doing."

"She doesn't know anything. Get out of here."

Sara was silent until dinner. "He's got a lot of nerve. I'm going to a job fair at the Coliseum tomorrow. Let's see what I can get. Let's move somewhere warm. I want to live in a house. I'm sick of our apartment."

Sara's best job offer came from Cooper County Hospital. It was a 48 bed facility in Mosley Georgia, sixty miles North of Atlanta. Sara could be the only anesthesiologist for the 30,000 residents of Cooper County.

Sara and I visited Mosley once before we moved. Sara had the potential to increase her income 2000%. She thought she could retire in ten years.

We liked the informal atmosphere. Everyone seemed friendly. I found one angry person, while I was pushing Amelia's stroller around town, waiting for Sara to get out of a meeting.

John Jefferson stood in a doorway with a portable microphone, speaker and sign. He ranted about "protecting the purity of our children." Nobody was paying attention to him.

Sara got the job. We rented a spacious house on an acre, one mile from the hospital. We lived there for six months before buying a seventy acre farm, ten miles away.

I asked our Jewish real estate agent about the racism. "Don't worry. If they come, we can all fit on one bus," he said.

The Census listed one Black person. Everyone said, "He moved."

Before the bus arrived, I bought a new Colt .45 and two boxes of bullets at the pawn shop on Main Street. Confused by the form, I asked the clerk if "psychiatric hospital" included "28 day programs." He replied, "Just sign it. I will fill it out later."

Churches ran all the local pre-schools. Amelia spent days with Brenda. Brenda promised, "not to teach her the Bible."

Brenda lasted until her husband invited me to join the local American Nazi club. I told him I was Jewish. He drawled, "I'm sure we got plenty of Jews there. But they don't talk about it much during the meetings."

Mrs. Fletcher, a retired elementary school teacher, replaced Brenda. She tutored Amelia on weekdays from nine until noon.

Mrs. Fletcher's morning lessons and afternoon assignments had Amelia reading at a sixth grade level when she was five. Amelia owned over two hundred books. We ordered books from catalogs, because the nearest bookstore was thirty miles away.

I took Amelia out on Saturdays, so an exhausted Sara could sleep. Wherever we went was an "adventure."

I was not prepared for Cooper County, although I lived in Brooklyn for twenty years, where everyone was certain they had seen everything. This was a typical Saturday.

Our neighbor Bill would stand in our driveway at 8 A.M., waiting for me to notice him. I made sure Amelia was occupied. I told her I would be right back and went outside to greet him.

Bill was 5'9" tall, stocky with a weathered/tan face. He wore overalls, a plaid shirt and a white baseball cap with "Smart Ass White Boy" printed in large red letters.

He always had a cheek full of chewing tobacco. I went inside his house once. There was a strange smell, because his wife was cooking possum stew.

Bill's ritual began with his favorite racist rant.

"After White men came to America, they had to kill the Indians, who were unclean savages, to protect their wives and children.

America was wonderful until greedy people wanted slaves. They forgot about history. They brought over more unclean savages. Now we have to clean up America all over again."

I interrupted his chuckling. "Got a rabbit?" Bill kept eight or ten beagles in cages. The cages were on a wooden platform, on his side of our private road. A caged rabbit was on an adjacent picnic table.

Bill removed the rabbit and stroked it until it was calm. Then he rubbed its fur against the beagle cages. The dogs went wild. He carried the rabbit to a meadow and released it.

The rabbit ran straight ahead. Bill opened the other cages, seconds or minutes later, depending upon his mood. The beagles instinctively chased the rabbit. I rooted for the rabbit. Bill's beagles were much faster.

After the chase, Amelia and I began our adventure in my new pickup truck. Unlike my neighbors, I did not purchase a see–through Rebel flag for the rear window, or store a shotgun there. It was common to see an unlocked truck, in a public parking lot with a long gun on a rack.

Our first stop was the closest store, Smith's Gas and Grocery. It was a mile from our driveway, but sort of around the corner.

Mr. Smith stayed inside. He sold almost everything. His fortyish son Luke, worked outside at the two gas pumps. Luke pumped gas, washed your windows, checked your tires and fluids.

Luke always made a fuss over Amelia. I thought it was cute. Sara said, "Keep Amelia away from Luke. I'm a Doctor. Listen to me." We went inside for the weekly newspaper and sugarless gum.

What's an adventure without a new toy? Next stop was K–Mart or Wal–Mart. On Saturday mornings there was another stop, at the only traffic light.

A fellow in a KKK robe, with his hood pulled down, held out a cup for donations. Every car stopped to drop in a bill or change. Political correctness in Mosley required a "Well, all right" – emphasizing the last word, before leaving. Traffic slowed to a crawl, but nobody honked.

I preferred Shoney's for lunch. Amelia never waited for food from their immaculate twenty–foot–long salad bar.

Shoney's parking lot was next to the Southern exit of Route 18, the main road from Atlanta. Mosley is located one exit North of Lake Henry Peterson, named for a Confederate poet.

Lake Peterson is busy during the Summer. It was important for tourists and minorities not to miss its exit.

Drivers with Cooper County license plates had a higher speed limit than others – especially drivers from other States.

A police car waited near this exit during the Summer. Another police car with a radar gun was on the highway.

As Amelia and I were leaving Shoney's one Saturday, an out–of–state Black man driving a brand new Blazer full of fishing gear, innocently pulled off the highway.

He stopped on the shoulder and stuck his head out the window. He might have asked the policeman, "Can you please tell me how to get to Lake Peterson?"

I anticipated a problem, because I had not seen a Black person for a year. After the policeman got out of his car, Amelia and I joined locals ambling over to this racist event.

The policeman shattered a headlight with his night stick. "You may not drive this vehicle. It is missing a headlight."

I understood the driver's frustration. However, I knew two things about Mosley. Keep quiet when unsure. Otherwise say, "Well, all right."

Alas, the driver said, "But." The policeman swung at a second light. "You seem to be missing both headlights." He strolled toward the trunk and smashed the tail lights.

"Please step out. This vehicle must be towed. You are charged with operating an unsafe vehicle." Driver said "But," before he was handcuffed and led into a police car. Police car and crowd left as another police car arrived, to protect the purity of this public place.

An enforced rest period for Amelia followed lunch. Sara and Amelia had their own adventure before dinner, riding on Sara's antique Ford 8N tractor.

We usually ate weekend dinners at Diner's Delight. Because "women who graduate from an American medical school never have to wash dishes."

Diner's Delight was the most popular restaurant in the area, open only on weekends. There was no menu, male waiters or unhappy diners.

Waitresses served iced tea and a variety of fried food. Diners requested additional bowls of items they liked. Everything except cole slaw and rolls was deep fried.

Diner's Delight meals began with bowls of fried chicken livers covered in corn flakes, cole slaw, and rolls. They served the best fried chicken I ever ate.

Sara drove us home after dinner. We always read a story to Amelia before she went to sleep.

Sara and I ended our day relaxing on our back porch.

Imagine the background noises of the jungle in a Tarzan movie, accompanied by the occasional sight of a burning cross on a neighboring farm.

Broken Red Light

Sara and I developed "The Anesthesiologist's Companion." It was the first practice management system designed for anesthesiologists. My first demo was in two weeks. I hoped to sell the marketing rights to a medical equipment company in Atlanta.

Sara was using our system for five months. I finished the last feature, an "ad hoc report writer," requested by Sara's billing company.

Our plumber Hank finished installing a sink in my new office bathroom, a few minutes later. He pointed to an old pool trophy on a shelf. "No damn Yankee can beat me at pool."

Amelia was with Mrs. Fletcher, Sara was working. I took a ride to Hooter County with Hank in his 1962 Plymouth Valiant. Hank drove ten miles to an illegal bar with two coin–operated pool tables. It was my first visit to Hooter County.

Hank stopped on a back road. I bought a half–pint of peach moonshine from a stand in someone's driveway. Hank had a six pack of light beer, in a plastic cooler that separated us on the front seat.

Three more roads brought us to a trailer. Two fellows were sitting outside on folding beach chairs. Rufus the owner, was speaking to a friend. Hank said his friend was race car driver "Wildcat Hootie from Hooterville" Jenkins. Rufus had no problem with my jar. I ordered a light beer for Hank, two sodas, and three dollars in quarters. I used up the change in an hour, beating Hank in five out of six games.

Hank took a different route home. He wanted to show me the main roads, in case I ever wanted to return. All I saw were fields and fences. The clouds and Hank's car were the only moving objects.

We traveled South on Route 18. This six lane road could take us to Atlanta, the closest thing to Manhattan around there.

I was staring at the clouds. Were my former Manhattan neighbors seeing the same clouds? A red traffic light blocked the intersection of Routes 18 and 260. It was the only traffic light I saw all day.

There were no cars in either direction. Route 260 was a two lane road. We could take it to pan gold in Dahlonega. Tall weeds on the Northeastern corner of the intersection blocked our view. The intersection was silent. We should have been able to hear a car.

"Well, I'm just gonna step on it," said Hank.

I convinced him to wait another minute. We timed it on his watch. No cars passed. We could not see anything. It seemed stupid to sit there. It was stupider that we did not get out of the car to check for traffic.

Hank finally stepped on his gas pedal. I expected to have a clear view of Route 260 in the center of the intersection. I could only see the front of a new Ford pickup truck, heading for my door.

I started to say, "Hank, we're going to get hit."

Hank's car took a direct hit, in my door. This formerly pristine car is now displayed on a junkyard's hill. My open window prevented a shower of broken glass. I was lucky Hank's car did not have seat belts, because I was able to move laterally.

The big truck squashed the little car in half. The impact pinned my left jaw against the right side of Hank's steering wheel. My right foot had been resting on the dashboard. A powerful force bent my right leg in half, the wrong way. My toes had touched my thigh.

Hank was not injured. His plastic cooler broke my left ribs and cushioned Hank. One ruptured beer can sprayed the interior.

A popular preacher and his two teenaged daughters, were in the pickup truck. They were not wearing seat belts. The impact ejected them through their windshield. The father and one daughter died at the scene.

The next thing I remember is sitting on the ground, watching an EMT cut off my blood soaked pants leg. But I could not feel my other leg. I wondered why he was treating the wrong leg.

The ambulance started moving. I said, "Hank? Are you still alive?"

"I'm okay."

"Let me touch your hand."

Hank's hand was warm. It calmed me. I let go and took a nap.

I woke up in a familiar place, outside Good Samaritan Hospital. The only hospital in a twenty–mile radius had a new name.

I knew everyone at the hospital, because I taught the staff how to use Sara's new operating room charts.

Sara designed them with room for extra information, and I printed them. Everyone liked them except the O.R. nurses. But documentation wins medical malpractice lawsuits.

Sara did not learn this stuff by osmosis. We never ordered cable television. We spent evenings reading thick books in our wonderful water bed. I read programming books. Sara read medical books. Sara's books were always thicker than mine.

Dr. Webb, the radiologist, was leaning over me. He must have been standing near the door when my ambulance arrived.

Dr. Webb gasped when he saw me. The last thing I remember is smiling and saying, "Don't worry. I'm too mean to die."

Dr. Webb thought I was delirious. He panicked and overdosed me on morphine. Sara said he almost killed me.

I don't know if I had a near–death experience. This is what Sara told me after I woke up.

Sara was not in the operating room, when Dr. Webb told her I arrived in an ambulance. She passed a handcuffed Hank before he went to jail. Police charged Hank with vehicular manslaughter. They released him after he passed a sobriety test.

Sara reversed Dr. Webb's morphine with Narcan. Sara said her operating room could not have handled me. She called Ray, her favorite general surgeon. General surgery is the greatest of all medical specialties.

Ray reserved an operating room at Monument Hospital, in Atlanta. Sara commanded her favorite EMT to drive us. She kept me breathing in the back of the ambulance with a rubber bag.

It was hard to breathe, because I ruptured my diaphragm. Ray fixed it. He closed the incision with a dozen staples. Ray did not allow Sara to be my anesthesiologist.

I woke up in the intensive care unit.

Sara's presence comforted me. She bought a cot and air mattress to sleep next to my bed.

It was great to be alive. It was annoying to find a tube in my throat. The dozen staples in my chest pulled in a dozen different directions when I tried to sit up. My right leg felt like dead weight. My fingers explored painful stitches on my left side, from a tube inserted during surgery.

A nurse told me I was in the hospital, and the long tube down my throat was helping me breathe. She handed me a paper and pad to communicate. I was breathing fine. I shook my head. I began coughing out the tube so I could speak. Sara shooed the nurse away, and removed the useless tube.

I did not care why my left jaw was loose. I wanted soft hospital food.

It was 11:45 on the wall clock. I said, "Lunch?"

I recall this conversation, because it was the only time I saw Sara shocked. She looked like Dr. Webb for a moment. Sara pointed to the dark sky outside the window. My next meal would be breakfast.

Sara adjusted my bed to let me sit up without pulling on my staples. She sat on a chair and smiled.

"Do you remember our trip to Florida last month?"

Fort Lauderdale was our favorite vacation spot. The lunchtime synchronized swimming exhibitions at the Swimming Hall of Fame were captivating. Sara and I also enjoyed attending Yankee games during Spring Training.

We took our last Spring Training trip without Amelia, because we wanted privacy to make her a baby sister. I nodded while picturing old Yankee fans with zinc oxide on their noses.

"You can't die. I'm pregnant. Our baby will need a father."

Nobody gave orders better than Sara.

Cataract Day

Amelia had no friends. She occupied herself with Barbie dolls and books. She rarely left our farm, except for drives to restaurants and stores.

Amelia wanted to go on vacation at the Jacksonville Beach Suites. Our little genius recalled her experiences at this hotel, three years earlier.

But Sara and I were too busy for a vacation. Sara was the county's only anesthesiologist. I worked for an orthopedic surgeon on weekdays, while Mrs. Fletcher was with Amelia. The surgeon and I created a system to test athletes for their pre–disposition to common injuries.

Sara was not a racist. Sara was always cordial to immigrants who learned English. She said, "Anyone who's smart, would want to learn English and move to America."

One of these smart immigrants was Dr. Juan Gomez. Dr. Gomez was born in Mexico. He lived in Roswell, near Atlanta.

Dr. Gomez could have attended the local medical school in Guadalajara. Instead, he learned English and borrowed a fortune to attend Emory Medical School.

Sara gave Juan her highest praise. "Juan is fast, but he's careful."

Tuesday was "cataract day" in the operating room.

Dr. Gomez searched nursing homes for potential cataract patients. Two vans transported these patients to Cooper County on Tuesdays. I forget how Juan found Sara. She provided the operating room, he provided the patients. Sara said, "All I have to do is show up."

Half of the patients returned for a second operation. Juan's cases provided over a third of Sara's income.

I had to pickup my visiting father at Hartsfield Airport on a Tuesday morning. Amelia and I followed Sara to the hospital. Amelia enjoyed eating at one of the six tables in the staff dining room. Dr. Gomez approached us at the end of our meal.

Dr. Gomez was short and slim. He had a thin face topped by a thick head of wavy black hair.

Juan was wearing greens, carrying a clipboard with the schedule. A blue cloth string around his neck held eyeglasses with powerful telescopic lenses.

Juan walked to Amelia. She smiled when he kneeled down to her level. He lifted her chin and seemed to be examining her eyes. "You have a beautiful daughter."

I corrected him. "My wife and daughter are the two most beautiful women in the world."

Juan turned to Sara. "You have a wonderful husband."

Sara said, "I'm not stupid," before taking a sip of coffee.

Juan and Sara started reviewing their schedule after Amelia and I said "Goodbye."

Sara came home twenty hours later. Amelia wore out my father. Dad was sleeping. Amelia, fresh from a six hour nap, was playing Junior Scrabble with me.

I knew something was wrong. It was the longest day Sara ever worked and the only time she did not kiss Amelia when she arrived.

Sara went directly to the quart of single–malt Scotch on the kitchen counter. She poured four ounces into a short glass and swallowed it. She refilled her glass and sat on the couch.

Sara took another sip of Scotch. "I'm going to get sued."

Amelia interrupted. "What is sued? Does this mean we can go back to the wonderful hotel in Florida? It's okay if we can't live there forever. And we don't have to go to the gift shop every day. Please Mommy, I want to go back there soon."

"Sued means I have to speak to a judge in court, about a man named Elmer Turner. Mr. Turner came to the hospital today, to get his eye fixed."

"What happened to him, Mommy?"

"A special person, Tom, the recovery room nurse, watches the patients after an operation. Tom's job is to make sure they are healthy. But Tom left Mr. Turner alone. Tom went to the bathroom.

Mr. Turner's brain was damaged, because he could not breathe for a few minutes. Mr. Turner is alive. He can talk, but he can't remember his name."

"Can't someone give him a new name? Elmer Fudd is a better name. It will be easier for him to remember."

"Mr. Turner's wife won't let him have a new name. She is also upset because Mr. Turner doesn't remember her name."

"Mommy? Why can't Mr. Turner watch cartoons all day? Then he won't have to talk to her. Mommy? Would you let Daddy change his name?"

Sara finished her Scotch and finally smiled. "No. I will change my name if Daddy does anything stupid."

Amelia turned to me. "Daddy, you better not do anything stupid!"

Amelia forgot about the Turners and Scrabble. She got up and went to her room.

I sat on the couch and held Sara's free hand. "Please tell me what happened."

Sara put down her empty glass and explained. "Tom is our only male nurse. They hired him three weeks ago. He's a competent nurse. But he thinks he's G–d's gift to women. Today, he stepped in front of me on his way in. He said, 'Doc, I know you want me. I can wait.' I pushed him back, as hard as I could.

He was wearing a sleeveless shirt, and I saw a swastika tattooed on his shoulder. I said, 'My husband is Jewish. Why would I want you?' This was his way of getting even. He'll get fired. I won't have to see him."

Sara saw Tom in court three weeks later.

Tom testified, "I asked her if I could take a ten minute break. She said, 'Sure'."

The judge believed him. Mrs. Turner became the wealthiest woman in Cooper County.

Amelia and I were playing Stratego when Sara came home after the verdict.

"I lost. The hospital suspended me for two weeks."

Sara sat next to Amelia. "I have good news and bad news. The judge said I made a mistake. The hospital does not want me to work there for two weeks. The good news is I don't have to work. We can live at the wonderful hotel in Florida for a whole week."

Amelia leaped up and kissed Sara. "Can we please leave right now? Oh Mommy! I hope you get sued again soon!"

Royal Palms

People complain about Wednesdays, "the hump day." Mosley residents considered it a good day to go fishing. All the stores on Main Street, except the bank, closed on Wednesdays.

One Wednesday morning, Mrs. Fletcher asked me if a book arrived at the Post Office. We received our mail at the Post Office, because Sara did not want a mailbox on the road.

Amelia said, "Daddy! You must drive to the Post Office right now. It's not cold. You don't need a coat. Go now!"

Amelia was a natural orderer. I obeyed her.

Amelia's book had not arrived. I decided to drive home through Mosley, Cooper County's only incorporated town.

Mosley was usually tranquil. Nobody honked their horn unless they were about to crash into your car.

I turned left at the end of Route 96, to drive through town, but a white pickup truck blocked traffic. A see–through Rebel flag covered the truck's rear window. Its horn played the first eight notes of *Dixie*.

The shirtless driver reminded me of Rambo, including the bandanna. He was standing on his seat, sticking out of his sun roof. He turned right to face the courthouse, pumped his massive arm and screamed, "White Power!"

After I pulled up to truck's rear bumper to get a better view, I saw John Jefferson standing in his regular spot outside the courthouse.

Jefferson was powered by hate and a battery-powered amplifier. He complained about racial integration on the side of the courthouse for an hour, two or three times a week.

Jefferson advised listeners to "protect the purity of your children." He sounded the same, with or without an audience. I never heard a heckler, only supporters.

Jefferson wanted enough supporters to serve in the U.S. House of Representatives. He was a smart fellow, despite his vitriolic rhetoric.

The racist Rambo tried another blast of *Dixie* and a louder, "White Power now!"

John Jefferson ignored him. Drivers in the other lane turned off their cars, and leaned out of their windows. Watching racist events was a popular pastime in Mosley.

The police car guarding the purity of our three-block-square downtown, turned on its light and siren. Our policeman drove in the middle of the road, to park next to the driver's window.

"Excuse me son, you're blocking traffic. You have to move."

"One second," said the racist. He faced Jefferson. "Jefferson! Show me White Power now!"

This event ended when John Jefferson raised his right arm.

Sara thought we could retire if we lived in Cooper County for ten years. Racist incidents made me want to leave.

We spent three steamy days in Fort Lauderdale without Amelia last year, to get away from the racism.

Our daughter Helene was born nine months after our vacation. Nurses delivered Helene because Sara's obstetrician was late. It was a fascinating birth. Sara gave orders to the nurses during labor.

Amelia treated Helene like a living Barbie doll. Amelia trained Helene to use the toilet before she was a year old.

But we could not raise school–age children in Cooper County. We were sitting on our porch one evening, watching a burning cross. "Darling, we've been here long enough," said Sara. "Where would you like to live?"

"Fort Lauderdale, Darling. Don't you want to live there?"

Moving was easy. Sara found an anesthesiologist to replace her. Our neighbor Bill, bought our farm. We bought two inexpensive camper tops, and filled the truck beds with our favorite possessions.

Amelia kept a dozen dolls and fifty books. We put a car seat and a child in each vehicle and drove over 700 miles to Fort Lauderdale. Our daughters alternated cars during rest stops.

Somehow, we forgot to research our destination again.

Normal people would not move 700 miles with two young girls, no prospects or a place to stay. We had great confidence in our abilities and $20,000 in traveler's checks.

Sara wanted to register with an agency for *locum tenens* work – temporary medical jobs. She expected to fill in for anesthesiologists who were on vacation. I expected to find a programming job.

First, we needed a place to live.

We answered advertisements from the newspaper in our hotel room. Everyone wanted us to move in at the beginning of the month, until we spoke to Charles.

Charles managed Royal Palms, a Lauderhill subdivision of eighty attached two–bedroom townhouses.

We arrived an hour early for our appointment with Charles. A dozen drug dealers and customers mingled on a corner, three blocks away.

Sara parked in the guest area. Our daughters sat in a double stroller. Helene had to sit in front, or she pulled Amelia's hair. We began an adventure, exploring our potential new neighborhood.

Half of the houses were empty. One of the two pools was dry. We met two female neighbors with three children walking to the functioning pool. Both adults said they liked living in Royal Palms.

Our potential neighbors on one side, had "Go Away!" printed on their doormat. Everything else seemed nice. It was different than Mosley.

Charles is the palest person in Florida. He wore a white shirt under a two piece khaki suit, and he carried a small briefcase, with the latest portable phone from Radio Shack.

His ex-wife chased him in a pink Mary Kay Cadillac. Charles, a consummate salesman, paused as he passed us. He said, "I'll be right back," before racing to the door of his townhouse.

The Cadillac jumped the curb through an empty parking spot. The driver swerved when she saw us, tearing out chunks of two small lawns. She skidded to a stop in front of Charles's townhouse, a foot away from Charles.

His ex–wife stuck her head out of her Cadillac's window and glowered, before screaming, "You owe me alimony. When are you going to pay me? You'll have to pay for my lawyer if I go to court. I want my money today!"

She was a good screamer. Sara studied her.

"Please let me rent this apartment. I will give you whatever I make," said Charles.

Sara nodded at me. Sara despised ineffectual men. She sympathized with his ex–wife.

The bedrooms were upstairs. Sara said we needed a gate to prevent our little darlings from falling down the stairs. I busied myself with our daughters and let Sara handle Charles.

Charles put on his best salesman's smile. He pulled two papers out of an attractive leather bound clipboard. "Isn't this a wonderful place for your family? I have a two year lease here, for you. The rent is only $600 a month. It will rise to $625 next year. I can cross that out.

Your rent will not go up. Please don't tell your neighbors about this. I would like you to rent this apartment. You seem like a nice family.

This is the best apartment you will find at this price. May I please get your signature on this? You can move in today. I need first, last and security. Today is the fourteenth. You can pay rent on the fifteenth, instead of the first."

I was retying Helene's shoe, trying to stay out of it. I heard Sara take a deep breath and braced myself for her bellow.

"You had a lousy lawyer. Why did you agree to pay your wife more money than you can afford? She still loves you.

She would not get upset if she didn't love you. Don't you understand? If you had any brains, you would get on your knees and beg her to see a marriage counselor with you."

Sara looked down at Charles. I swiveled the stroller so we could watch the woman we loved.

Charles sobbed.

"When are you going to start counseling, Charles?"

Charles fell down. He curled into a fetal position, holding his ankles.

Sara kneeled and lifted his chin. "Are you going to do that today?"

Charles wailed. I could not understand him, but he satisfied Sara.

"We'll take this apartment for one year, at $575 a month. We will pay our rent on the first, like everyone else. We will pay you $300 now for the rest of this month. We are not paying security or the last month's rent in advance," said Sara.

Charles muttered "Okay." His pants were dry.

Charles had a lease ready with Sara's terms, when she handed him three traveler's checks. He handed her keys and a temporary pool pass.

Florida was not what we expected.

Holiday Rent–A–Car paid me $8 an hour to edit spreadsheets. But Florida wanted Sara to be a resident for six consecutive months, before she applied for a medical license.

"I am going to find something different to do. Let's not tell anyone that I am a Doctor. Darling, let's do better research before we move again."

Sara tutored our daughters for a week, before applying for a job. Sara claimed to be a stay–at–home Mom.

She got a commission–only job selling aluminum siding over the phone from six to nine PM. Her sales increased every week. Sara claimed it was an acquired skill. She made everything look easy.

Charles traded an empty townhouse, two doors away from us, for the part–time services of a young fellow.

Charles wanted Jim to replace broken shingles on all the roofs. Jim had a house and job for at least three months.

Amelia and Helene woke us one Sunday, to take them to the pool at 8 AM. We met Jim, starting his first day of work.

Jim was tall, muscular, tanned. He had long straight brown hair pulled back into a ponytail and the longest beard I saw in Florida. Jim's blue eyes matched his Grateful Dead t–shirt, cut off denims and bright blue basketball sneakers. He carried a tool belt over one shoulder and a ladder over the other. Jim clutched the handle of a half–gallon bottle of Vodka in his right fist.

Sara asked Jim, "Have you ever worked on a roof in Florida?"

"No. I've been working as a gardener. I did lots of roofing in North Dakota, before I moved to Florida."

"Florida is hotter than North Dakota."

Jim put everything down. He sprinted into his house. Jim returned, smiling, carrying a small knapsack. He showed Sara two plastic bottles. One filled with water, the other empty, for a urinal. "Thanks. I almost forgot my other bottles," he said.

While he was picking everything up, Sara said, "It will be over a hundred degrees on the roof."

"I'm strong. I can take it. I can go home if I get hot."

At the pool, Sara said, "If you want to get drunk, drink with me or drink in a bar. Don't drink on a roof in Florida."

"Why?"

Sara dismissed my question with a wave. "Did you see the way he looked at the bottle? He couldn't wait to start drinking. He won't last two hours. It's 8:15. You can expect to hear an ambulance before ten o'clock."

Sara was correct.

The door to Jim's townhouse was open when we returned from the pool. I saw Charles inside and joined him.

Jim slept in the downstairs living room. A portable TV was on the floor, in front of a multi-stained mattress. Jim used a rolled up denim jacket for a pillow.

The room smelled from beer because there were about twenty empty beer cans next to Jim's mattress.

"How could a roofer fall off a roof? I never should have hired him," said Charles.

I went home and prepared tuna salad sandwiches. We heard another ambulance while I was selecting ripe mangoes for dessert.

Sara said, "Charles."

Sara liked Charles, because he thanked her for encouraging him to speak to a marriage counselor with his ex–wife.

It wasn't Charles. Brian, our morning lifeguard, overdosed on barbiturates. Brian fell into the deep water. He almost drowned while his assistant was smoking marijuana in the bathroom. A twelve–year–old boy put a float under Brian's neck and kept Brian's nose out of the water until his assistant returned.

I asked Brian about it when I saw him. "You know those new Russian tenants? The man and wife? I taught her to float on her back. Her husband came over to thank me for helping his wife. He shook my hand and put something in it. I expected a ten or twenty.

He gave me blow. I snorted it in the bathroom. It made me sweat a lot. Then I saw Marabel, the tall one with orange hair. She always takes pills. I thought they were Valiums. She sleeps and sets an alarm to turn over. I took two of her pills, and woke up in an ambulance. I can't understand why Charles didn't fire me."

Sara left me with our daughters while she went to a new beauty parlor. Amelia and Helene asked me to read *Snow White*. I was a more interesting reader than Sara, because I read all the characters in different voices.

Our doorbell rang, before I started reading. Two unwashed children were waiting for me.

"May I help you?"

"My name is Jodie. This is my brother Timmy. I am five and Timmy is three. We live next door."

"Where?"

Jodie pointed to my right. They lived in the townhouse with the "Go Away!" welcome mat.

"We're hungry. Can you please make us something to eat? Our parents are out. Grandpa is watching us. He's not allowed to cook."

"Why?"

"He burned down our old house the last time he used the stove."

I supervised Jodie and Timmy while they washed their hands. I served them peanut butter sandwiches, milk and vanilla wafers. Amelia and Helene watched them eat. When Jodie finished, she asked if Amelia and Helene could watch TV next door.

I made a peanut butter sandwich for Grandpa, and left a note for Sara.

The townhouse next door was immaculate. I sat next to Grandpa while my daughters and their filthy friends raced to the TV set.

"Hi. I'm Bruce. Thanks for the sandwich. I forgot to eat today," said Grandpa.

Bruce was filthier than his grandchildren. It took me a moment to get used to his odor. Bruce's clothes smelled like urine. His breath smelled like the whiskey he was drinking from a water glass. A fifth of Winslow was on the table next to him.

Bruce devoured his sandwich. "Please do mc a favor. I'm a little drunk. Please help me walk to the door so I can smoke. I'm so ashamed to ask for your help, but I'm not allowed to smoke inside."

Bruce was about 70, 5'7" tall, 120 pounds. I wrapped my left arm under his bony shoulder for the ten steps to the door.

Bruce seemed fine leaning against the building. I brought him a chair, ashtray and his glass. Bruce finished his drink before Sara arrived with a short haircut.

I complimented Sara on her short hair style, before introducing her to Bruce.

Jodie used the remote control to find a pornographic movie. Helene said, "Look Daddy! That Mommy is not wearing any clothes."

I turned off the TV. The children went to Publix with me.

Sara bathed Bruce and changed his clothes while we were shopping. She was on the living room couch watching CNN when we returned. I unpacked two grocery bags before joining her. Sara turned off the idiot box and kissed me.

"I'm glad we don't have cable TV. CNN's news, the people in it, the reporters, their subjects, gets stupider every time I watch it. How was Publix? You look tired."

"Four children are harder than two. Can you please make dinner?"

Sara tossed me a deck of cards. "I counted them for you. See if you can entertain the children without a TV."

I bellowed, "Who wants to play Go Fish?" Four children came running in from another room yelling, "I do!"

After three games of Go Fish, I went next door and returned with Candyland.

Bruce sat on a chair outside, next to a portable snack tray for liquor and tobacco. I poured whiskey into a Kool Aid pitcher, the one with the smiley face, added some water, and left it on Bruce's tray. I joined Sara on the couch. Sara held a finger to her lips and nodded toward the children.

Sara appeared to be reading *TV Guide*, the only book in the house. But she was listening to Amelia offer her interpretation of Candyland's rules. Amelia added new rules, because her new friends could not read the rules on the box.

Bruce bellowed, "Hey! You watered it down. Get over here." He waved me over and whispered, "There's a case under the table."

I returned with a half–pint of straight stuff in the Kool–Aid pitcher. Bruce tasted it. "Perfect! Why don't you have one, while the missus is inside?"

I avoided answering his question, when a black, two–door Camaro skidded into the parking space in front of us. Bruce said, "Timmy and Angie. My son and his wife."

The Senior Timmy preferred "Tim." Tim was tall, skinny, covered in black: black t–shirt, jeans, referee shoes, large sunglasses. His contrasting head was covered with short bleached blond hair. A tattoo of "Tim" under a halo, drew my attention to his right forearm.

Tim rushed by me without acknowledging my presence. My little angels were safe because Sara was nearby.

Angie reminded me of Anne Francis as Honey West. She was five feet tall, a hundred pounds. Angie wore almost the same black outfit as her husband. Jet–black hair poked out of the rear of her black baseball cap.

She was trying to remove an enormous black gym bag from the rear seat. I felt a stirring in my loins, watching her bend over in her form–fitting jeans. Bruce snapped me out of it. "She's a looker!"

I offered to help her. Angie pointed to the gym bag, so I carried it into her house. Tim was returning with an empty box from a large television set. He said, "I met your wife," as he passed us.

In her house, Angie looked around. She said, "Put it anywhere," and went outside to her car. I placed the bag on the floor and shrugged at Sara before I followed our new neighbor outside.

I was too late to help. Tim was rushing back with his box. Angie was closing the trunk after removing two small shopping bags.

Angie pointed to a puddle under Bruce's chair. "It was easier than getting up," said Bruce.

Angie closed the door behind Bruce and locked it after we entered. They sat at opposite ends of the dinette table.

Tim and Angie shook powders from two pill bottles on small makeup mirrors. "Give us a minute," said Angie. They inhaled their powders through the matching gold straws they wore around their necks.

Sara thought drug users should become physicians, to get the real stuff.

"We rob houses," said Tim. "We're out all night sometimes. Thanks for helping Grandpa. We had to move because he burned the last place down. Don't worry. It won't happen again."

I watched Angie inhale more powder while I waited for Tim to mention his children. They were not his little darlings.

"I want to go to sleep," said Angie.

Tim shook my hand. "Thanks for helping with Grandpa." They entered their bedroom and shut the door.

Bruce needed liquor.

I added one ice cube to a half–pint. "Why did you put ice in here?" said Bruce. He moved the ice cube to his ashtray.

"Hey Bruce. Does anyone ever help you with your grandchildren?"

Bruce laughed. "Oh no! Tim and Angie don't like visitors because of their business."

Amelia was watching a National Geographic rerun, the other children were playing Candyland. Amelia left after winning the first game, because Helene insisted upon reading the rules on the box to her new friends.

I asked Sara if we should adopt two neglected children. "Not on your life. We need a plan," she said.

Sara told the youngsters they were having a sleepover next door. She led a surprised Jodie and Timmy to their bedroom for pillows, pajamas and an optional doll. Sara packed everything in a plastic garbage bag. Angie and Tim remained in their bedroom.

Amelia, alone in front of the TV, asked, "Daddy? May I please stay in my room?"

"Sure. Let's go to Publix first. You can get a treat."

Amelia chose Oreos. She was usually limited to vanilla wafers, because Sara said sugar makes kids stupid.

I bought tuna, American cheese, microwaveable breakfast sandwiches and frozen chocolate cheesecake.

Amelia never whined or begged. She behaved better than most adults.

Barbie brought out the little girl in Amelia. Amelia loved everything about Barbie. If I felt like annoying my wife, I would ask Amelia what she wanted to do when she grew up. Amelia always replied, "I want to be like Barbie."

Back in Georgia, Sara once said, "What have I done wrong? How could she read all those books and still want to be like Barbie?"

I asked Amelia to write a story about Barbie. I thought Amelia would develop a new interest, if we pushed more Barbie into her life.

Instead, Amelia presented us with a captivating story.

Barbie's Mommy was the most intelligent person in the world. But lightning struck Mommy while she read *Cinderella* to her only child.

Barbie was sad. Her Mommy said, "Barbie, go to India. Ask Mother Teresa how to find happiness," before she died. Mother Teresa advised Barbie to visit sick children in hospitals.

All the sick children wanted to meet Barbie.

Barbie healed thousands of sick children with her smile, without touching their diseased bodies.

One day, the President got sick. He kept getting sicker. Finally, his only intelligent assistant asked Barbie to cure him with her smile.

The President met Barbie. He recovered when he saw Barbie's smile, and asked her to marry him.

They got married after he agreed to let Barbie replace him as President. "Everyone would rather have a beautiful President," said Barbie.

Barbie became the best President. She never needed advice because she knew everything. Barbie banned Presidential elections, to be President forever. Everyone lived happily ever after.

Amelia wrapped each page of her story in plastic wrap, and taped it to her wall. Sara had to see it whenever she was in Amelia's room.

Sara won our coin–toss to pick Amelia's name. She wanted to name her after Amelia Earhart or Marie Curie. Amelia won out, because Sara feared Marie might sound foreign.

Sara did not like most foreigners.

Sara was never nice to physicians who graduated from a foreign medical school. Sara explained, "If they're too stupid to get into an American medical school, they're too stupid to practice medicine here." Sara annoyed me with this once.

It happened in St. Donna's pharmacy. Sara needed antibiotics, but physicians are not supposed to write their own prescriptions.

Sara ordered a pharmacist to ask someone working in the Emergency Room to write it for her.

A beautiful intern, with a red dot painted on her forehead, delivered Sara's prescription. She said, "Hi Doc. I'm on break."

Sara examined the paper before she asked, "Where did you go to med school?"

"University of Bombay. I'm from India."

Sara turned to me. "Darling, Bombay is full of rats. The Indians killed all the snakes that ate the rats, to export their skins. The city is now infested with rats."

The intern said, "We are working diligently to solve this problem."

Sara faced her. "I can understand why you would want to leave an impoverished, vermin infested country.

But this hospital should have higher standards. They should not hire doctors who graduated from an Indian medical school."

Sara showed me the difference in requirements for American and Indian medical schools. Americans do about twice as much work as Indians.

The resident might have thought this was a test. "I am a very good Doctor."

"You can't be a good Doctor. You've had no education. You speak English well. You didn't go to an American medical school because you were too stupid to get in. Right? Am I right about this?"

"Yes! You are correct. The Indian entrance exam was much easier."

Sara turned to me. "If I wasn't around, would you let anyone who did not graduate from an American medical school, examine or treat Amelia?"

"Did you marry an idiot?"

Sara shook her head. The resident was gone.

Our American pharmacist said, "I don't understand why they hire foreigners. I went to an American school, like you."

"Like me? How are you like me? You went to pharmacy school. You were too stupid to get into a real school, like me.

We used to have real pharmacists. They were helpful. They knew how to prepare medications. You don't have to do anything.

When was the last time you prepared anything? You read directions, measure water and powder, put it in a bottle. What else can you do? You can count pills. You're a pill counter. Please count me fourteen pills."

After a subdued pill counter returned, Sara said, "Thank you." She took the bottle and turned to leave.

The pharmacist said, "Excuse me," while Sara sucked in another breath.

"Were you going to ask me to pay for this? I work here. I don't pay for anything."

Sara never paid for medical treatment. Only one physician complained: the obstetrician who arrived late for Helene's delivery.

Sara bathed Jodie and Timmy, and dressed them in pajamas.

Amelia went to her room. Helene watched *The Little Mermaid* for about the thirtieth time, with her new friends. Young children love repetition. They want to know what will happen next. Surprises scare them.

Sara arranged blankets and pillows on the living room floor. All the children were comfortable. She distributed bowls of microwaved popcorn to the happy children.

I returned from eating two semi–frozen pieces of cheesecake in the kitchen to find Sara and Timmy asleep. He was young enough for a nap. I wanted a nap too, but somebody had to be the responsible adult.

Our doorbell rang before I had to watch *The Little Mermaid* again. Sara stirred. I waited for her to sit up before I opened our door.

"My name is Penny. I live across the street. My husband Keith is hurting me. Can you please help me?"

Penny was in her early twenties, 5'6" tall, auburn hair, sunburned fair skin. She weighed at least 200 pounds. A torn t–shirt, exposing a plain white bra covered her torso. "Thunder thighs" showed under short, cutoff jeans. Penny was not wearing shoes.

Sara sat Penny on the couch and sent me next door for a cup of Bruce's whiskey.

Sara began her examination after Penny had two sips of whiskey. The exam ended when Sara pointed to a red circle on Penny's thigh. "Did Keith do this to you?"

"He burned me there yesterday, with his cigar."

Sara snapped to attention, and held Penny's hand. "Please do something for me. I am calling the police. When they get here, please tell them he burned you today. Will you do that for me?"

"Will Keith get in a lot of trouble?"

"Do you want him to do this to you again?"

"No."

Sara walked to the kitchen and called the police. I watched Penny sob and wondered why we were living there.

Police sent an unmarked car to our townhouse. Sara met the police outside and showed them her Georgia medical license.

Two handsome policemen in their early thirties got out of the car. One Black, one White, each about 6 feet tall and 200 pounds. I had never been this close to a Florida policeman.

The Black policeman carried a clipboard and a stack of forms. He spoke to Penny, she signed forms. His partner spoke to Sara in the kitchen. Police ignored the children and me until Sara and the White policeman returned. He said, "Let's go."

We did not go far. A young White guy was outside. Keith was in his mid–twenties, short and slim. He wore a sleeveless t–shirt, gym shorts, cheap white running shoes.

Keith made a poor first impression, drinking from a can of beer while he walked to us. Keith asked the policemen, "Is my wife in there?"

The Black policeman responded. "Sir, you should not be drinking beer in public."

Keith ignored him. He shouted, "Penny are you in there? I want you to come home."

The White policeman said, "Sir. Please pour out the contents of your beer."

Keith grimaced as he poured out his beer. Charles walked toward the disturbance.

The Black policeman said, "Sir, can you please show me identification? I would like to ask you some questions."

The White policeman continued. "Sir? Please show me your identification."

"I don't mind talking to you," said Keith. He pointed to the Black policeman. "I'm not talking to him."

The Black policeman handcuffed Keith three seconds later. If ESPN held handcuff competitions, he might win.

As a police cruiser arrived, the White policeman asked Penny, "Are you ready to go?"

Penny hesitated until Sara said, "Do you want to stay married to him?"

"I never should have rented to him," said Charles.

We went home. The Little Mermaid was ending. Sara answered our phone. She agreed to work in the morning, to fill in for a sick employee. I agreed to stay home with our daughters and their friends.

I called in sick before I microwaved breakfast sandwiches for my brood. Jodie said, "This is my Mommy's favorite food." As if by telepathy, Angie rang our doorbell.

Angie wore a classy yellow sun dress and smelled great. If house thieves tested perfumes, she picked a great one. Angie walked right by me to the kitchen. She seemed surprised to find children eating her favorite microwaved sandwiches.

"Good morning everyone. Take your sandwiches to the car. We're going to visit Aunt Connie."

I packed their belongings back in her garbage bag and carried it to her car.

"Thanks for watching my kids," said Angie. "We have to leave Florida. It's better if you don't know where we're going."

"Aunt Connie's," I said.

"You're nice. Call me when you're ready to leave your wife. Bruce has the number."

The telephone was ringing when I went inside. An employment agency called with a better job than Holiday. There were other applicants and they wanted to interview me ASAP. I said I would go to the interview if I found a babysitter.

I pondered my predicament while I took out the trash. Looking across the street, I noticed Penny's next–door neighbor. He was a White male about 35, entering his townhouse with two small children. His children were about the same ages as Jodie and Timmy. I could not understand why I never saw them before.

I waved, and jogged across the street. "Hi! Can I please speak to you for a minute? I have two young girls and I got called for a job interview. I was wondering, since you have well behaved children, if you could please watch mine for an hour, two tops. My wife is out selling aluminum siding. I'm stuck."

His children pushed each other, trying to get in the door first. I liked this fellow because he was calm while he separated his little angels, a boy and girl.

I returned with my little angels. A woman walked in, carrying a bundle of newspapers. She introduced herself as Ellen, Archie's wife. Archie apologized for not introducing himself.

They were both mid–thirties. Archie was about 6'2", 240 pounds, with a gut. Ellen was a foot shorter and weighed half as much as her husband. They were both wearing white t–shirts and cut–off jeans. If Angie was half as attractive, and not wearing makeup, she might look like Ellen. Archie was bald, with a Navy tattoo on his right bicep.

Archie said he worked in the printing department of the Sun–Sentinel newspaper. He was home, because he severed the tip of his right pinkie on the job. Archie hoped for another two weeks of disability payments.

Ellen, like Angie, was carrying in heavy objects from her car. Ellen picked up advertising sections of the Sun–Sentinel from her husband's job. She sat on the floor, cutting out "two for one" coupons, for items sold in drug stores.

Ellen bought products from CVS, because they doubled all coupons. She resold everything at the Flea Market on Route 441.

They seemed more normal than yesterday's neighbors. I checked out a bathroom. Their house was okay.

Archie allayed my fears with his last three questions. He asked about allergies and for Sara's work number in case of an emergency.

Archie paused before his final question. "Do they like to play Candyland?"

I smiled. Archie said, "Who wants to play Candyland?" as I closed the door.

My interview was a bust. I counted eight people on line for one $11 an hour job. There were three job seekers ahead of me when I left.

Driving back, I thought of wonderful places to visit with Sara, if Archie turned out to be a good babysitter.

I parked and strolled across the street, savoring my last seconds of kid–free time on this beautiful day. Amelia opened Archie's door. The other three children were watching cartoons.

Amelia whispered, "Be quiet, Daddy. Archie is sleeping. The telephone rang and he did not answer it."

I closed the door while Amelia returned to the cartoon show. Archie was reclining on the couch. He wasn't sleeping. He was dead. There was a red silk scarf wrapped around his left bicep. A hypodermic syringe was in his arm, below the scarf.

I kept Archie's death a secret, until I saw Charles and his wife across the street, getting out of her pink car. Despite the current mess, I enjoyed seeing them together. I waved to Charles and motioned for him to cross the street. I said, "There are four kids in the living room with the renter. He died of a drug overdose."

His pale face turned pink while he stared at Archie. "I never should have rented to him," said Charles. "It used to be nicer around here." Then he collapsed.

"Why is everybody tired today? Daddy, you must tell them to go to sleep earlier tonight," said Helene.

Charles's chances of survival increased when Sara's truck arrived. I bellowed, "Sara!"

Sara sprinted across the street, and sat on the floor next to Charles. Sara opened his collar, and removed a PaperMate pen from his pocket. She opened the pen, and removed the refill. Charles gurgled after she thrust the point of the refill into his neck.

"Sonny, call 911. Say 'I have a code, and I need a bus.' And bring me a clean towel and a straw."

Charles's ex–wife ran across the street when the ambulance arrived.

She asked Sara, "What's your name?"

"Sara. Without the aitch."

"Thank you for saving Charles. It's about time he rented to nice people. I'm pregnant. Charles doesn't know. If it's a girl, I want to name her after you."

She joined Charles in the ambulance.

Ellen arrived, with a car full of products. Ellen ran inside without them when she saw the ambulance. Sara blocked her. Sara held her arms and whispered, "Your kids are okay. Your husband oh–deed. Police will be here soon."

Sara released Ellen and nodded in my direction. I loaded a daughter on each arm and followed Sara home.

"Daddy, can we please watch Cinderella? Jodie left it here. Can we please watch it once before we give it back to her?" said Amelia.

I humored her, on this humorless day. "Sure. It's a great movie."

Amelia looked both ways for Mommy. "I would like to grow up to be Cinderella instead of Barbie."

"Do you ever want to grow up to be a Doctor like Mommy?"

"Why? I just want to be beautiful."

Sara was not home.

I found Sara and Bruce sitting beside his snack tray with drinks. Bruce waved at me. "Hey! Come here. Quick! Help!"

"What's wrong, Bruce?"

"Please take your wife home. She is scaring me. She said I have to wear diapers. If she sees me sitting in a puddle, she will call someone who will put me in a home, where they won't let me drink."

Sara stopped him with a wave. "Darling, please drive to CVS and pickup two packages of Depends. Get one medium and one small for Bruce."

Bruce started to say, "But," when Sara silenced him with another wave.

"You're going to wear diapers buddy, and there's nothing you can do about it."

Nobody gave orders better than Sara.

The Boy Never Came Back

We lived in Royal Palms until our lease expired. It was Sara's turn to choose our next location. She chose Atlanta.

Sara got us day jobs at the Stone Mountain Hospital Emergency Room. I helped her colleague digitize medical records while Sara treated patients. We needed two software upgrades before the voice recognition system understood the staff's Southern accents.

Sara rented an impressive house on a half–acre of Emory Road, near the medical school. Amelia and Helene attended an expensive private school. Most of the parents were a physician or attorney.

A week later, we heard Amelia use a racist word to curse Helene. Amelia said her classmates used the word.

Sara and I quit our jobs and moved in with my parents. We rented two parking spaces for our trucks.

On our second day, I found an immaculate antique stroller next to the garbage cans on East 13th Street. I brought it upstairs on the elevator. Mother said, "It's like yours. It brings back good memories," before she walked to her bedroom.

Mother returned wearing shoes for the first time in years, to take Helene to the Homecrest Avenue playground, two blocks away.

"It's almost time for lunch," said Dad.

"I will make tuna and cheese sandwiches."

"I'm going to take a snooze. Please call me when lunch is ready. Don't forget to make me a tea with lemon."

Sara read *Weekly World News* while I watched *The Price Is Right* with Amelia. At the end of the show, Amelia set the table with Barbie plates and napkins while I made lunch and coffee.

Sara put down her newspaper when I brought her coffee. "Want to wake Dad? He is always happy to see you."

"Are you sure?"

Amelia waved at Sara. "I'll wake Grandpa. I will be nice. He is my favorite Grandpa."

Amelia returned a moment later. "He's still sleeping."

"I better get him. We will never hear the end of his complaints, if he missed lunch because his wife wanted to go outside."

Dad was dead. I washed my tears off in the bathroom, before I returned to lunch.

"Let him sleep," I said.

Amelia cleared the paper plates off the table. She loved throwing things into the incinerator chute down the hall. She created more garbage when she returned by washing her hands and drying them with paper towels. Amelia said, "May I please watch TV?"

Sara nodded to Amelia. I nodded to Sara and led her to my deceased Dad.

I asked, "What do we do about Mother?"

"I'll handle her. Take two leftover sandwiches from lunch. Sit with her until I get there. Leave me the Rabbi's phone number. I'll get everything taken care of before you see me at the park. Keep your Mother out of here."

I hugged Sara. "I am glad I married you."

"Don't ever forget it. Get going."

I packed four juice boxes with the sandwiches. I found Mother and Helene sitting on a bench near the swings.

Mother looked up as if she expected to see me. "I got dizzy from pushing her on the swings. I had to sit down."

Helene said, "It's okay Daddy. Grandma's dizzy."

We were silent until Mother stood up. I got a chill as her eyes widened. "Everything turns around and around. It won't stop. It won't stop."

Mother sat down and faced Helene. "It stops in a minute."

I opened a juice box and handed it to Mother. "Sara told me to drink juice if I get dizzy."

Helene wiped her brow. "Whew! I worried for a minute. Or maybe a second. It's okay Grandma. Daddy can bring Mommy over if you need a Doctor right away. If you can wait until I'm 25, because Mommy says I have to be 25, I will be a Doctor. Then I can help you instead of Mommy."

"I thought you wanted to be beautiful like Snow White, so the Seven Dwarfs could take care of you," I said.

Helene stood up. "Mommy made me promise. Mommy said I must be useful. She said Amelia can only be beautiful. I have to be a Doctor and take care of Amelia when she gets old and stops being beautiful. I don't mind."

"I feel much better," said Mother. "Your wife is always right."

"I have more juice and sandwiches."

"Not now. More swings, Helene?"

Helene reached for her hand. They walked to the swings.

I sat on the bench, waiting for tears, until I felt Sara's hand on my shoulder. Amelia sat beside her.

Sara said, "I signed the death certificate. The Rabbi called a hearse. The police wanted to poke around. I got rid of them. I gave my key to the Rabbi to lock up. He wants you to be at Schneider's Funeral Home by 10 AM."

Sara waited for me to nod. "What are we going to do with your mother?"

"I have an idea. Follow my lead."

We walked over to the swings. Mother pushed Helene high, saying "Whee!" with each shove.

Amelia said, "I want Grandma to push me. Is this a bad time?"

I put a finger to my lips. It was the first time I saw Mother out of breath. "Whew! I was dizzy for a minute. I'm better," she said.

"The water at the apartment house is not working. Dad is staying there. Why don't we go to Uncle Ralph's for a while? He's never met Helene."

Uncle Ralph is Mother's only sibling. He lives nearby, in an attached two–family house.

"My no–good brother," said Mother. "Grandpa gave him everything. I had to work full–time so he could go to college. Now, he never calls me."

I watched Mother spit for the only time in my life. Sara handed her a tissue. Mother wiped herself before she continued.

"And his miserable no–good wife. Everyone thinks she's Kosher. She orders spare ribs from Chinese takeout, and eats them on paper plates with her bridge club."

I gasped for Mother's benefit.

"Tuesday nights. Mim eats spare ribs every Tuesday night."

Mother lowered her voice. "I know things about certain people."

Helene asked, "Do you know anything about me, Grandma?"

Mother replied, "Not now. I'm thinking about things. It's Tuesday. Let's go visit Ralph. Let's see if his wife eats spare ribs while I'm around."

I was speechless until Mother said, "What are you waiting for? I'm tired, let's take a cab. I haven't taken a cab in years. Go find one. Helene and I will wait on the bench."

I left Sara on the bench. I tried to carry Amelia, but she was too heavy to carry for a block. Luckily, we found a cab passing on the corner.

Mother said, "I'll ring the bell. I wonder when her bridge club gets here."

Ralph and Miriam lived on East 28rd Street. Their three daughters shared the downstairs apartment before they got married. A narrow staircase between the kitchens, connected the apartments.

Mother paused at the door. I handed her a juice box but forgot to unwrap and insert the straw. Mother said, "I'm dizzy. Don't expect me to do anything."

Ralph heard her. He opened the door while she was sucking on the juice box. "What are you doing here?"

Ralph and Mother were both 5 feet tall. She called Ralph "five by five" because he weighed over 200 pounds.

"Move away. I am dizzy. I have to sit down."

Ralph stepped aside. "You've been dizzy as long as I know you."

I waved to Ralph. Mother sat on Ralph's chair, the largest chair in the living room. Mother waited until we were all assembled.

"My water's not running. We're staying downstairs tonight. Make sure you have plenty of towels for my granddaughters. We can play Scrabble while your no–good wife eats spare ribs with her bridge club."

"They don't play here. Why is she my no–good wife?"

"I remember what she was like before you married her. Do you think I forget these things? Nobody would go out with her except you. Everybody wanted to go out with me and I was still a virgin when I got married."

"You've been here before. Go find your own towels. You can make hamburgers for dinner. We bought a side of beef. It's in a new freezer downstairs."

Ralph pointed to me. "I'll show you."

As we reached the freezer, I said, "Dad died today. Mother doesn't know. The funeral is ten o'clock. Will you go?"

"I knew it had to be something. He died in the apartment?"

"Yes."

"I might go to the service. I don't go to cemeteries. Aren't you living in Florida?"

"We moved from Florida to Georgia. We were planning to stay with my parents until we found a place in the city. Sara wants to live near her hospital."

Ralph squeezed my cheek and pulled my face down to his level. "You can stay here as long as you like. I'll give you keys to downstairs. Tell your mother to be nice to Aunt Mim or I will put her in the Golden Gate Inn. There is no reason for her to be nasty to my wife."

Ralph released my cheek. I said, "Thanks Uncle Ralph," and moved in for a hug.

He pushed me back. "People in this family don't hug. I'm going to watch the news in my bedroom."

I selected ground beef, the only meat Mother could chew. There were three beds. One for Mother. She would sleep alone for the first time in over thirty years.

Amelia and Helene watched TV in the living room. I found Mother and Sara in the kitchen.

Sara told Mother, "You must see a psychiatrist. I will get a recommendation from the hospital."

"I don't want to take anything that will make me groggy."

"They have wonderful new drugs that don't make you sleepy. Will you try this?"

"I'll try it. But I want something different if I don't like what he gives me."

"It won't be a 'he.' I want you to have a female psychiatrist."

"A woman? Thank you."

Sara faced me. "Your mother knows what happened. She can live with us and be our new tutor. We won't have privacy. But we won't have to rush home before six. She's going to use your father's life insurance for a down payment on a four bedroom apartment."

Mother displayed a gruesome toothless grin. "You'll have plenty of privacy. I want to go places. I'll buy new clothes at Saks."

I said, "Do you have anything black for the funeral tomorrow?"

"I don't go to cemeteries. I can wear what I'm wearing to the service. If they don't like it, too bad."

"Do you need anything from the apartment?"

"Get me his life insurance policies from the top drawer of the file cabinet."

"Anything else?"

"We both had our idiosyncrasies. I put up with his, he put up with mine. He's gone. I can do whatever I want."

Mother turned to her granddaughters. "Put on channel 24, CNBC. Then bring me a big yellow pad and pencil from the table in the kitchen. Sit with me. I am going to teach you all about the stock market. You can help me pick stocks so I can get rich and buy us all beautiful clothes from Saks."

Amelia said, "What is Saks?"

"Saks is a wonderful store on Fifth Avenue, where Grandma shopped before she got married."

Amelia and Helene ran to the kitchen. Mother raised the volume.

I asked Sara, "Would you mind going back to the apartment with me?"

Sara walked over to Mother. "We'll be back in an hour. Please answer the door. Ralph's in his room."

I found a knapsack in my old bedroom. I filled it with spare clothing for our daughters and six juice boxes. Sara read the policies. Dad was insured for $460,000. He had a $250,000 policy, a $200,000 policy and a $10,000 policy from the Army.

I brought Mother's address book to call our relatives.

Our last stop was a liquor store for two quarts of whiskey.

Helene opened the door.

"Guess what Mommy and Daddy? We're having an energy crisis. Don't have a crisis. A crisis is bad." She shook her head while we followed her to the living room.

Mother pressed "Mute." "Hand me those policies. Then hang up your suit so it's not wrinkled tomorrow."

"I brought your address book. Is there anyone you want me to call?"

"No. You know who to call."

"Does Ralph still have the separate number downstairs?"

"How should I know? Call it. See if it rings."

Amelia pointed to the TV. "Grandma, look! It says 'Bulletin'."

Mother waved at Sara and me. "Leave us alone. We have to concentrate."

Sara and I sat in Ralph's downstairs kitchen. She said, "Don't worry. She'll never get her hands on the money. In New York State you need two signatures to certify that someone is insane. I'm one of the signatures."

I opened my bottle and took a deep slug.

Sara said, "Go easy. I want to talk to you later. You are having a crisis. I'm here for you. Why don't you make those calls and take a nap? I'll wake you for dinner. First, come here."

Sara stood up and held out her arms. I cried while she held me.

"Don't worry, Sonny. I will always be here for you. You are my one true love. Don't ever forget it."

Liquor helped me make phone calls. Uncle Jerry was driving from Philadelphia. I stopped after calling my cousin David. He couldn't make it because it was "a bad day."

Sara woke me at midnight. She handed me a tray with a hamburger, glass of water and three aspirins.

"I let you sleep. You better eat this. You need strength tomorrow."

I took a swig of whiskey and forced myself to eat.

"Your Aunt Mim is a pip. She's the only sane person here. She said your father used rope for a belt before he got married. Your mother bought him a new wardrobe from the Sears catalog."

I laughed. "Everything except shoes. Dad always wore Murray Space Shoes."

When I finished eating, Sara said, "I read them a story. Say 'Good Night' to your daughters."

I kissed a sleeping Amelia. Helene was reading Sara's *Weekly World News*. "Don't worry, Daddy. It's a crisis. I know it will be better soon," she said.

The New York news from a clock radio woke me at 6:30. I showered and was upstairs twenty minutes later. Mother slept on Ralph's chair in the living room.

"Help me up. I'm stiff. I fell asleep watching a movie. Hurry up. I have to go to the bathroom."

I waited for her to return.

"Are you going with me?"

"No. I changed my mind. Tell everyone I didn't feel good today. On your way back, get a dozen danish from the bakery. I feel like something sweet. My five–by–five brother always wants something sweet. Make sure you don't get anything with nuts."

I stared at her, wondering how Sara would react to my death. Mother said, "What are you waiting for? Time marches on."

I kissed her and left.

Walking to the subway cleared my head. Chris's Bar was down the block from the funeral home. I stopped in Have–A–Nosh, and ordered six scrambled egg sandwiches for the bar.

I arrived at Chris's five minutes after opening. I wore a suit and carried the sandwiches. Chris, studying *The Racing Form* at a table, received the first sandwich. Mike, Joan, Don and Fred got the remaining sandwiches.

Mike placed a dark Winslow and ginger ale in front of me. He said, "That's with me," before I took a sip.

"Top of the morning," said Joan. "Sara sent you out to find a job. Good for her. Good for the nerves to have a drink before an interview. My father had a drink before work every morning. He kept the same job for 43 years."

"Thanks for breakfast. Now I can go straight home and sleep," said Fred.

"Whatever Lola Wants," sang Don. "I hope you are getting a job in Brooklyn, so you can come here and drink with your friends. Don't ever forget you're from Brooklyn, the greatest place in the world. Is there any reason to go anywhere else? I only go to Manhattan to see shows. Otherwise, I stay right here."

"I'm going to Schneider's in an hour for my father's funeral."

Joan waved to her husband. "Honey, he needs another one. His father died. He's going to Schneider's."

Mike poured another glass, three–quarters full of straight Winslow. "I am always here to serve mankind in times of distress."

Mike whispered, "How did he go?"

"Dad took a nap before lunch. When I went to wake him, he was dead. Sara's with my mother and the girls."

I drank half of Mike's drink. Mike replaced my ginger ale with water. "Better stick to water. Sugar might make you sick later. How much time do you have?"

"An hour and a half. It starts at ten but I want to be early."

I felt a hand on my shoulder. "I heard funeral," said Chris. "Who?"

"My father took a nap. He didn't wake up. He was 72."

"I'm 72. Did he drink or smoke? Was his heart OK?"

"He smoked for six months in the Army, because they gave him free cigarettes. He drank beers once or twice during the Summer, sitting in the parking lot with his friends. He was fine."

"I don't like to hear bad news." Chris handed me a card and pen. "Write down your mother's name and address. I will send her flowers. You're family around here."

Chris added, "Your wife, too. Let me know if you need anything. You can leave your kids with me for an hour or two before I go to the track. I can feed them and read stories."

I forgot my germophobia and shook his hand. "Thanks Chris. I appreciate it. I know my mother will appreciate your flowers."

Chris waved at Mike. "I've got a ride coming. Watch 3, 4, 6, 8 in the late triple. They're all long shots."

Mike said, "Wait," and searched the top of the cash register for a blank piece of paper.

Don interrupted, "3, 4, 6, 8. I can remember."

Chris said, "You? You can't even remember the second line of those songs you sing."

Chris patted my back. "This is the best place to be. We're your friends. Your wife too."

Joan put her arm around my shoulder and planted a wet kiss on my left cheek. "I'm going to the funeral with you. I've been to plenty of Jewish funerals. I know what to do. It's better to get there late. Otherwise, you'll have to listen to a lot of stuff you don't want to hear."

I asked Mike's wife, "Are you sure? Won't they think you're my mistress?"

Mike pointed to Joan. "Woman! Return to your seat."

He refilled my glass before he announced, "I am here to serve mankind, womankind and kidkind. But I will not serve my wife if she misbehaves."

Joan picked up her drink and coaster. "Ha! You better serve me. Because if you don't, you don't want to come home tonight."

"Yes, woman. I will obey you."

Joan startled Don by touching his shoulder. "Huh?"

"Switch seats with me."

Mike refilled my glass. He poured himself a drink and held it up to a sliver of sunlight. "I am here to serve mankind, womankind and kidkind. I will let nothing, not even a misbehaving wife, deter me from my duties."

Joan picked up her empty glass. "What are your duties here?"

A beet–faced Mike said, "Oh, never mind."

"Wait."

"Yes, woman, whom I married 28 years ago and have grown to love more each day."

"I'll have what he's having."

Joan and I left the bar at 10:15. Uncle Jerry grabbed my coat sleeve as we entered Schneider's. "You're late. Who's this? Your mistress?"

He moved his nose next to my mouth and sniffed. "Are you drunk?"

"Nice to see you Uncle Jerry. This is Joan. She offered to join me. Mother and Sara stayed home with the girls."

Rabbi Frey appeared while Joan and Jerry shook hands. "You're late. Why didn't you come to the morning service? Who's this? Your mistress?"

He handed me Sara's key, five papers and a pen before I could reply. "Sign this. We had the service in the lobby to save you money. You have two death certificates, and the bills for the box and burial."

Rabbi Frey sniffed Joan's lips before bowing. "Hello. I'm Rabbi Frey."

I asked Uncle Jerry, "Can we please ride with you?"

"Of course, nephew."

It rained during the half hour drive to Old Montefiore Cemetery in Queens. Uncle Jerry had two golf umbrellas in his trunk.

Rabbi Frey handed me a prayer book. "Page 272."

I motioned to Jerry. He shook his head. Joan and I shared an umbrella. She held the umbrella and my arm, breaking only when I shoveled dirt into Dad's grave.

I returned the book to Rabbi Frey at the end of the service. He said, "I hope I see you at 7:30 tomorrow morning."

Uncle Jerry left Joan at the bar before driving to Uncle Ralph's house. He handed me a mint before we walked up the stairs.

Amelia answered the door. "Hi Uncle Jerry. Hi Daddy."

Jerry patted the top of her head. Amelia took his hand and led him inside. Mother was watching the ticker tape on CNBC. "Jerry! I wasn't expecting company."

"I'll only stay a minute. Do you need anything?"

"Look at all these people here. How could I need anything? How's your wife?"

"Pearl died two years ago."

"I'm sorry. We should talk more. I'll call you."

Mother added "Call Jerry" to the notes on her pad, as he left.

She said, "I knew things about Pearl. Jerry was the only one who would go out with her. They made fun of her in school. Oh well, we all die sometime."

Mother pressed "Off" before continuing. "It's no fun without real money to invest. I'm giving you and Sara half, for a down payment on an apartment. I'll put the other half in the market.

We need income. Sara must finish her surgical residency. I know things about her. She never liked anesthesiology."

Mother stood up. "Don't worry. They're all nice things. I have to go to the bathroom. Then I'm going to teach Amelia the multiplication tables. I'm their new tutor.

I got a hundred on every test in elementary school. I can teach them everything I learned. I can't teach anything after ninth grade, because I had to work full–time. My granddaughters will be able to do anything. I hope they can skip high school when I'm done tutoring them."

Mother handed me a scrap of newspaper titled, "Youngest Harvard Student." He was eleven. The previous record was twelve.

"Read this article. His parents tutored him. He never went to school. You could have done it. I didn't realize it then."

I found Sara and Helene napping downstairs.

Helene woke up. "Come here, Daddy. I have to hug you. I made Uncle Ralph hug me. He didn't want to."

Sara got up and waved her hand. "Were you in Chris's bar? Change your clothes."

"Joan went to the service. Jerry drove us to the cemetery. Joan was helpful. They were good company."

"Sorry. Take a shower and talk to me in bed. You stink."

When I returned, Sara asked, "How was Joan? Did everyone think she was your mistress?"

I laughed. "How did you know? She might enjoy fooling around while her husband is working. I like Joan. Would you mind if I met her once a week?"

Sara laughed before she lifted my chin, to look into my eyes. "I like Joan. You can fool around with her as much as you want. But don't fall asleep."

"What do you mean?"

"Do you remember the Zelda Miller case?"

"No."

"Rich, older woman. Her young boyfriend kept her in a coma with insulin, while he spent her money."

"Is that what you would do?"

Sara dismissed me with a wave. "You don't have any money. Why would I want to keep you around? I would get a double–oh needle, zero zero, the smallest one."

Sara caressed the side of my neck. "After you fell asleep, I would fill you with enough insulin to kill you. It wouldn't be found in an autopsy. I'd inject it into one of these marks on your neck. No one would see the needle hole.

I still have a New York license. I can write a prescription and keep a syringe by the side of the bed."

Sara removed her hand. Her eyes turned black, an evil grin contorted her face. "Want me to go out and get this now?"

"No. I won't sleep with Joan."

Sara patted the top of my head. "Good boy. Take a nap. I'll wake you for dinner."

"Wait. Mother wants to give us $230,000 for a down payment on an apartment, and replace Mrs. Fletcher. She wants to invest the rest to support us, to help you finish your surgical residency."

"Your mother is correct. I called St. Donna's. They want me back. Let me talk to her. She needs medication."

Amelia recited multiplication tables at dinner. Aunt Mim said, "She learned multiplication in one day? Ralph, when did our daughters learn multiplication?"

Uncle Ralph replied, "I don't remember," and kept eating.

"Don't forget Mim, your daughters didn't have me as their tutor."

Aunt Mim pointed to me. "What about him? He had you. He went to Brooklyn College like everyone else."

"I know things now that I didn't know then. I know things about you, Mim. I don't feel like discussing them now."

"I know things about you. But I won't say them in front of your son."

"I could tell you a lot of things about your no–good husband."

Ralph interrupted. "Please stop arguing. I'm tired of eating hamburgers and scrambled eggs." He nodded at Sara. "How long are you planning to stay here? A ballpark figure is fine."

"Two weeks. Your sister is giving us the down payment for an apartment. I'll start looking for one tomorrow."

Sara pointed to me. "You have to drive your mother to two insurance companies."

"I won't go in his truck. It's too hard to get in and out."

"Please take my car," said Ralph.

"It's about time you're doing something nice for your only sister."

Mother swiveled in her chair. "Amelia, you can watch TV. Helene, please help me clear the table. Then I am going to teach you subtraction."

Helene walked over to Sara. "Mommy, I'm going to learn 'traction'."

"The word is subtraction, baby."

"The name is not important. And I'm not a baby. Grandma said I can go to Harvard College soon. They don't let babies go there. Right, Grandma?"

Mother replied, "I don't feel like discussing this now."

Sara and I went downstairs. I finished yesterday's bottle before I relaxed on the bed. "I will never have another drink."

Sara sat on the bed. "What brought this on?"

"Chris's Bar. I went there on my eighteenth birthday. Maria, she was Rudy's girlfriend, bought me shots of Jack Daniels until I threw up. Why did I go back?

I wanted drinks before the funeral. Everyone was on their best behavior. Chris volunteered as a babysitter. He wants to read stories to our little darlings in the rear booth.

Chris is sending flowers. He mentioned you. Don and Chris said they were my family."

Sara held me when my eyes got moist.

"I don't want them for a family. I don't want anyone to think Joan is my mistress. I want different friends in a different place. What do you think?"

"It's a good idea. Maybe I'll stop too. I don't want to consider the possibility of your mother drunk. This way we won't have any in the house."

"What about Mother? Do you think this will work?"

"I don't know. I'll overlook the first two times she causes a problem. Strike three – she goes into a home. You and the girls can visit her.

I will try my hardest to make sure she takes her meds. But our daughters come first. I will not let her shenanigans jeopardize their safety."

"I promised my parents I would never put them in a home."

"Too bad. Anything else?"

"I need sleep."

"You've had a hard day. You need three aspirins and a large glass of water. Do you also want something to help you sleep until the morning?"

"I don't need it."

Sara returned with water and aspirins. "Drink it all. Give me a kiss. I'll see you in the morning. You are loved. Not at Chris's. Right here, in this house."

Uncle Ralph owned an 1963 Mercury Comet. It seemed too small for him to drive.

Mother explained. "Mim always drives. Ralph hasn't been able to fit behind the steering wheel for twenty years. He never liked driving. Do you want me to tell you some things about Ralph?"

"Later. Let's get in the car."

"I'll get in. Find me something to hold on to. Make sure you lock the doors."

Mother wore a purple dress she called a "moo–moo." One of Ralph's hats covered Mother's head, a pair of Dad's cataract sunglasses covered half of her face. She said, "I don't want anyone to know it's me."

Mother refused to sit on waiting room sofas. "Who knows who's been there? Maybe it was someone who didn't wash their hands after a bowel movement."

When we approached a receptionist, she said, "You talk to them."

"Dad died. I forgot Mother's medicine and she has a terrible heart condition. Could someone see her now?"

A moment later, a pleasant man wearing a stylish suit would lead us into an office and point to two chairs.

Mother waited until he sat before saying, "When was the last time someone cleaned this chair? And who was here before me? Never mind, I'll stand."

I complimented Mother after our second visit. "You were great. We spent less than fifteen minutes there."

"What did I do? Take me home. I'm going to have to go to the bathroom soon. Did I ever tell you about my friend Ruth Brown? She used to drive me all over the place. I never liked driving.

Ruth drove us to different places to eat, out on Long Island. I paid for our meals. Ruth was afraid of germs. She wouldn't go into a public bathroom.

One time we had to drive all the way home from the Hamptons when she had to go. You know what she did?

She stopped drinking. She would only drink at night after she got home. I told her, 'Ruth, you have to drink. You will get sick.'

I was right. I wouldn't ride with her after she got out of the hospital, because I was afraid she would die while she was driving. She died two months later.

Hurry up. Let me see how fast you can get there. Don't worry about getting a speeding ticket. It's Ralph's car. Let him pay for it."

"That only works with parking tickets, Mother."

"When we get out, I have to go to the bathroom, and you need something to drink. Don't become like Ruth Brown. Promise me you'll drink something.

I want to apologize to Ralph, for trying to make his life miserable for the past fifty years. But if Ralph starts up, I can't let him beat me in an argument. You know that, don't you?"

"You are the smartest mother in the world."

"Thank you. I wouldn't say I'm the smartest. Don't let Sara put me in a hospital or a home. She's got a mind of her own.

Oh look, there's Ralph's house. Be glad your father had insurance. We all have to go sometime. Now help me up the stairs."

Ralph opened the door. Mother said, "Ralph, I'm sorry for being nasty to you. Please move out of my way. I have to use the bathroom."

Ralph tugged my sleeve. "Aunt Mim got an idea. Take this check. We're going to invest $100,000 in your new apartment. Give us a share of whatever it costs."

I almost hugged him. "Thank you. Where's Aunt Mim? I would like to thank her."

"She's out bowling. She's in a bowling club. They go out for Chinese food. She's not home until ten. We watch the news and go to sleep. I hope you're sleeping okay.

I like something light to eat, maybe herring and crackers, before I get in bed. Otherwise, I wake up hungry in the middle of the night. Does that ever happen to you?"

I avoided answering when the doorbell rang.

Ralph looked through the peephole. "I don't know who it is. You better open the door."

A short Asian woman was nearly hidden behind an immense basket of flowers.

"Who sent this? It must have cost a fortune. I know what these things cost," said Ralph.

I showed the card to Ralph: "Best wishes, Chris."

"Who's Chris?"

"A friend of mine."

"He must be a good friend to spend $200 on flowers. What good are flowers? I have grapes and tomatoes in the backyard."

Mother saw the flowers when she returned from the bathroom. "Oh Ralph! Thank you for the flowers. You must have paid plenty for this. Are you making money in the market? What have you been buying?"

"They're from someone named Chris. Ask your son about him. We can talk about the market another time. I don't feel like it now."

"Who's Chris? Chris is not a Jewish name," said Mother.

"Chris owns a bar and a rooming house on Coney Island Avenue. Sara and I go there sometimes. I took Dad there once."

"You took my husband to a rooming house? No wonder he never wanted sex. Was this rooming house clean? Did he have his own bathroom? Are there prostitutes in this bar?"

"We went there once. We had one beer."

"Then what happened? Did he use protection? Do you have a brother somewhere who's going to show up asking for money?"

"Then we left. I can't remember if we walked home or took the bus."

"I went to a bar once with Ruth. We didn't stay long because she wouldn't drink. How does Chris make all this money?"

"I think he picked the first three horses for the last race at Belmont yesterday."

"I want to watch the market. I haven't seen it all day. Your wife is taking a nap with Amelia and Helene. She wants you to wake her up.

Please ask her to make me a cup of tea with milk and bring me six cookies. What are you waiting for? Get going. Don't forget a snack tray. Ralph doesn't like to leave it out in the living room. He thinks Amelia and Helene will knock it down."

I woke Sara. "Mother wants you to bring her a tea with milk and six cookies."

Amelia tugged on the side of my shirt, "Can I help Grandma?"

Helene tugged on the other side. "Can I cook something for her? I know how to cook things. Don't make it too hard, Daddy. A snack, not a whole meal. I hope she doesn't want a hamburger or scrambled eggs. Mommy? Can you please get Grandma new teeth from the hospital?"

"I will get Grandma teeth. Ask Uncle Ralph to make her tea with milk. Put six cookies on a small plate and setup a tray. Let Amelia help you.

Bring Grandma a snack tray with a spoon and napkin, while he's making tea."

"I'll get the snack tray, Amelia. You get the spoon and napkin."

"No! I want to get the snack tray. You get the napkin."

Sara said, "Stop. There are two parts to the snack tray. You have to do it together."

Helene punched Amelia's shoulder. "See? Mommy said we have to do it together. You aren't the Boss. Mommy is the Boss."

"Excuse me," I said. "Don't forget that I am a Boss too."

Amelia stopped rubbing her shoulder. She guffawed and slapped her thigh. "You used to be a Boss. Mommy's the Boss now."

Helene nodded. "That's right, Daddy. Only Mommy is the Boss now. Not you. Only Mommy."

Sara placed her index finger on my lips. "Would I ever tell them to do anything bad?"

"No."

She grinned. "So what's the difference who's Boss?"

Our daughters walked upstairs chanting, "Mommy is our Boss."

"Guess what Uncle Ralph? Daddy is not our Boss anymore, only Mommy," said Helene.

I asked Sara, "Where have I gone wrong?"

"You haven't done anything wrong."

"We should try for a son."

"Are you crazy? I'm not going through that again. And don't worry about your mother. I've been reading up on this. There's a new drug called Seroquel. I'm going to get your mother on it tomorrow.

An attending will examine your mother during her lunch hour. I don't want to move until we see if it works.

Let's give it two weeks. Your mother is comfortable here. Moving will be stressful. She must be medicated.

I'll drive her there. I bought a stool to help her get in my truck."

"If we're staying, Helene wants a stool to reach the stove."

"Forget it. She's too young to cook. I'm the Boss."

A week later, I found Mother in front of the TV, watching *All My Children*. I waited for a commercial before asking, "What happened to the market?"

"Forget the market. I put everything into municipal bonds. The market's too hectic. I can't understand it. If you see Aunt Mim, ask her if she wants to play cards with me. I don't feel like getting up."

Sara sat at the kitchen table with Uncle Ralph, solving the *New York Times* crossword puzzle.

"I traded a tutor for a sane mother, Sara. We have to enroll the girls in school."

"Try a public school first. There might be a good one near you," said Ralph. "You can always switch to private schools later."

"I didn't tell you, Sonny." Sara kissed my cheek. "I found an apartment. Eight rooms on the eleventh floor, with a river view."

"How much?"

"575."

"Yikes. We could get a nice house in Westchester for the same thing. They have better public schools."

"Forget it. I'm not living in Westchester. I want to be able to walk to work and Zabar's. I'm not thrilled about this public school idea, either. Public school kids come home with lice and the flu. But I will be there tomorrow, as an observer."

"I have to be at MIS by nine. Why don't you drive? Unless you want to try the express bus. It stops on Sheepshead Bay Road."

"It costs twice as much as the train," said Ralph. "But it is comfortable and quiet. The bus runs every fifteen minutes during rush hour."

Sara glared at me. "How about if I drive? You sit in the death seat with the girls in the back. We'll play a little game. I'll cut off the car on my right whenever you say 'bus'. There will be bumper–to–bumper traffic. It should be interesting."

"I've got a better idea. Instead of 'bus' I'll say 'Joan'. I could say 'Aunt Joan' for the benefit of our daughters."

Sara surprised me with a right overhand punch to my nose.

Ralph held Sara in a bear hug until she said, "I'm okay."

"Take it easy, Sara. You're under a lot of stress. Me too. I'm going to take a nap. Mim is in the backyard with your daughters."

Sara took my free hand, as I held tissues to my bleeding nose. "Keep your head back. I'm sorry."

Sara went to the kitchen for ice before she led me downstairs. "Get in bed. I want to look at your nose."

Sara examined my nose. "It's not broken. Keep the ice on it. I'll stay here with you. I'm sorry, Darling. I don't ever want to hurt you.

You are my one true love. I was kidding when I told you about the insulin. I've thought about it. You might fool around sometime. I spoke to my sister about it. She thinks men's bodies age differently.

You might want someone with a better body than me. If it happens, we'll go to counseling. I won't kill you. I am an anesthesiologist. I can stop your heart, if I want to kill you."

Sara grinned. "Of course, I could paralyze you and feed you through a tube. Then I could wake you once in a while, for extracurricular activities. If it worked out, I could share you with my friends."

Sara stretched out. I stopped her when she moved closer. "Didn't you take an oath to heal people before you graduated?"

"I never took an oath," she said. "I stayed home that day. But you're safe. I would need more drugs than I could steal from a hospital to keep you paralyzed."

Sara examined my nose. "You're still bleeding. Keep ice on it. I'll get a clean towel and more ice."

Amelia and Helene replaced her on the bed a moment later. "What happened, Daddy? Mommy said to keep you company."

Helene kissed me. "Did you fall down?"

"No. Mommy punched me in the nose."

"Why did Mommy punch you?"

"I told Mommy a joke she didn't like."

"Daddy did you tell Mommy a joke about…"

Amelia covered Helene's mouth and ignored Helene's follow–up punch to her shoulder. Amelia said, "Sex? Were you talking about sex?"

Helene tugged my hair to get my attention. "What's sex, Daddy?"

"It was not a joke about sex. If you want to learn about sex, go upstairs and ask Grandma to explain the 'whosis' and the 'whatsis' to you."

They waited for Sara to come down the narrow staircase. Helene said, "Grandma's going to teach us about sex."

"What did Helene want?"

"Helene thought you punched me because I told you a joke about sex. She wanted me to explain it. I told them to ask Mother about the 'whosis' and the 'whatsis.' That was how she explained sex to me."

Sara replaced my ice and towel. "Let's get something straight. You didn't tell me a bad joke. The only thing worse would be if my father popped out of my birthday cake.

Three things bother me: Bob, buses and the thought of you in another woman's arms. Can you promise not to mention any of them?"

Sara extended her hand. It was the only time we shook hands.

I said, "Can you please get us a new address? And enroll our kids in a school?"

"I don't know if I can do it all tomorrow. We need an address. I like the apartment on 103rd Street.

I don't like the elevator and doormen. It has manual elevators. We waited at least five minutes for the drunken doorman. He could barely stand up."

"It will be annoying to move the car for alternate side parking."

"We're not parking on the street. Let's sell your truck. I want to rent a space in the garage on 100th Street."

Sara examined my nose. "Wash your face, and go talk to your mother. I'll make dinner. I want to make it an early night. Find a movie we can watch after dinner."

Mother looked up from her chair when I arrived. She was taping flowers from Chris's bouquet on Amelia and Helene. "I'm glad you're here. Find me more tape."

Helene said, "Look Daddy. Aren't I beautiful? Grandma said she would buy me a new dress at Saks, so I will be more beautiful. I could be more beautiful than Amelia."

Amelia dismissed her with a wave. "Forget it. You'll never be more beautiful than me. I am the prettiest girl in the world. Nobody is more beautiful than me. You can be almost as beautiful as me."

"Okay. I don't mind being almost as beautiful as you."

"I'm getting a dress, too. Saks has everything," said Mother.

Helene said, "Grandma, can we please go to Saks on one day every week? It doesn't have to be the same day, just one day a week."

"I have to think about it. I haven't decided yet."

Amelia pushed me away. "Don't wait for her to decide. Go get more tape."

I found a large roll of electrical tape under the kitchen sink. Mother used it to attach the rest of the flowers. The girls taped three flowers to Mother. I used Mim's vacuum to remove the mess.

The noise alarmed Mim. "I never heard anyone using a vacuum in my house. I couldn't imagine what happened."

Ralph said, "Remind me to buy more electrical tape."

"I should remind you? I bought you a notebook to keep in your shirt pocket. Go find it and use it."

Mim pointed to Mother. "I hope you didn't let your husband get away with stuff."

"I never let my husband get away with anything." Mother pointed to me. "I never let you get away with anything, either."

Mim placed her hand on my shoulder. "It was for your own good."

Mother smiled. "Thank you. He doesn't appreciate what a wonderful mother he has.

Look at your daughters, Sonny Boy. I always wished I had a girl. You never knew. I wanted to dress you up in girl's clothes. Your father wouldn't let me. He got upset. I dressed you in white.

I made you wear white clothes, so you wouldn't want to get dirty. I yelled at you if you got dirty, until someone at your no–good school found out about it. A private school.

You'd think they would leave you alone and let you do what you want to your kids. No, they had to stick their nose into it.

I gave the white pants to the Salvation Army and bought you six pairs of black dungarees at Sears. I let you get dirty. But you didn't want to get dirty. I can't think about it now. I'm getting dizzy. Please help me up.

How long have I been sitting here? I have to go to the bathroom. Then I want a drink, so I don't become like Ruth Brown."

Mim said, "Ruth Brown. She had that beautiful car. What was it? A Cadillac?"

"A Fleetwood. It was better than a regular Cadillac."

"Does she live around here? I would like to visit her."

"She's dead. She stopped drinking."

"Wait. People die because they start drinking, not stop."

"No. She stopped drinking everything."

Mother sighed. "Ruth was nice. She sat behind me, all through elementary school."

After Mother left, Mim said, "Ruth was strange. I know some things about her and they're not nice."

Mim turned to our daughters, sitting in Ralph's chair. "Let's see what your grandmother did."

Mim attached more flowers with electrical tape. "Go show your father."

Helene asked, "Daddy, are we more beautiful now?"

"I'm not sure. Why don't you ask Uncle Ralph?"

Mim sighed. "I better see what he's doing. Older men can't remember anything.

Your mother never forgets anything. She's doing better now. She hasn't said anything nasty to Ralph since she started taking those pills."

Helene and Mim walked away holding hands.

Amelia was frowning. "Daddy, you didn't tell Helene a good answer."

"Why?"

"You told her to ask Uncle Ralph. He didn't see us before."

"How am I supposed to know if you're more beautiful now?"

"You don't have to get an attitude."

"I'm supposed to know everything."

Helene waved. "Don't be silly. Only Mommy knows everything. She's the Boss of this family."

We watched Sara's favorite movie, "Never Cry Wolf." It's about a fellow who camps in the wilderness with wolves.

Everyone liked it except me. I particularly dislike when the hero eats mice like the wolves. First he cooks mice, then he tries eating them raw.

Sara handed her bottle to me in bed. "Sit up and drink."

"I stopped drinking."

"I'm a Doctor. Listen to me."

I swallowed an ounce of Scotch. I said, "I do not understand why people drink Scotch," before I handed the bottle back to Sara.

Sara took a sip and returned the bottle. "Have another drink. You're more fun after you've had drinks."

The bottle was next to my lips when Mother, wearing only a slip, approached us. Mother sat on the edge of the bed. "Pour me an ounce into one of the paper cups from the bathroom."

Sara shrugged, and returned with three cups. Helene, wearing one of Amelia's old Barbie nightgowns, approached us. "What are you drinking, Grandma?"

Mother replied, "I don't feel like discussing it now," before laughing for the first time in ages.

"What does that mean Grandma?"

"Darling, say 'I do not feel like discussing it now.'"

Helene said, "I don't want to talk about it now."

"Perfect. Now you know the answer to every question in the world. Use it if you ever don't know an answer or don't feel like answering. It works all the time. Trust Grandma."

"Can I use it in school? I want to get a hundred on every test, like you."

"No. It didn't work in school. At least not when I went there."

Grandma took a sip and smiled. "It might work now. Things are different."

Amelia approached us, rubbing her eyes.

"Grandma, will it work on Amelia?"

"Of course, Darling."

Amelia whined, "Why did I hear my name? Why is everybody talking loud? It woke me up."

Helene said, "I'm sorry. I don't want to talk about it now," before running, screaming, back to their bed.

Mother handed me her cup and hugged Amelia. "I'll put you to bed, Darling. I'll sing you a lullaby to put you to sleep."

Sara refilled my cup. "Keep drinking."

I almost choked when I heard my soprano Mother, who took singing and piano lessons, singing opera. I showed Mother's cup to Sara. "She drank less than an ounce."

"I'm glad she doesn't have a problem with alcohol. We can have it around."

Ralph and Mim approached us, wearing matching green checked bathrobes. Ralph stuck his nose next to my lips. "Did you give her a drink? She only sings opera after she drinks."

"She had less than an ounce."

"And you let her have it?"

Ralph turned to Sara. "I'm surprised at you." He took Mim's hand and walked upstairs.

I had a wonderful interview with Roger at MIS.

MIS replaced six programmers with one consultant, since my last visit. The consultant fixed bugs described on "incident reports" from technical support.

Roger had new features planned. MIS did not want to release an update without new features.

Roger wanted to rewrite the system in C++. It was a new "Object Oriented" language based on C, the language I knew.

"I don't know C++. Why are you interviewing me?"

"Relax, nobody knows it. You know the system."

Roger handed me a brochure. "We're sending everyone to a one week course in Boca Raton."

MIS was an "IBM shop." MIS only used IBM hardware, software and services.

Roger showed me the new cubicles. All MIS employees, except Roger and Jessica worked in cubicles.

Roger grinned. "You can order any workstation you want. As long as it's in my IBM catalog."

My salary was more than doubled, to $65,000 a year. I did not have to report to the office for a month.

Roger agreed to reimburse me for my family's expenses when I attended the seminar in three weeks. "You have to stay at a hotel on my list. Jessica will have a fit if Disney World is on your expense report."

Roger gripped my hand. "Don't forget to bring your wife. Part of this salary is to listen to her on Fridays."

I smiled for an hour during the hot and crowded subway ride back to Uncle Ralph's house. I stopped at the florist on Neck Road and arrived with five small bouquets of flowers.

Ralph answered the door, wearing a well–fitted navy blue suit and a light blue bow tie.

"I hope none of these are for Mim. You'll spoil her. She'll expect them all the time, like she expects me to take out the garbage."

Ralph opened a wrapper and removed a carnation. He bit off most of the stem and handed it to me, before attaching the flower to his lapel. "Thank you. We're going to Roseland for the early bird special."

Aunt Mim painted two circles of rouge on her face. I said, "Hi Aunt Mim. You look great."

"Thank you. It would be nice to hear it from my husband once in a while. You brought flowers. Look at that, five bunches. You remembered your Aunt Mim."

Mim tilted my chin to look into my eyes. "Your mother raised you better than I thought. She wanted a girl. I better be quiet. I'll tell you another time."

Mother walked in. "Ralph, when was the last time you changed your shirt?"

Ralph said, "They all look the same," as he left with Mim.

I handed Mother a bouquet of flowers. "I got a job."

"You always get jobs. If you want to impress me, find more tape."

My family arrived.

Amelia was first through the door. "Daddy, we got a new apartment and a new school. Helene and I can go to the same school."

She handed me a brochure for the Manhattan Valley Montessori School. "This is the school. They have school all the time, but you only go for ten months. I met my teacher, Mrs. Carson. She was nice."

Helene said, "My teacher was not nice. I wanted her to call Grandma to remind her to buy me a new dress at Saks. She said it was not important for me to wear a new dress at this school. Why don't they want me to be beautiful?"

Sara said, "Sometimes you sit on the floor in Montessori School. The boys will see your underpants if you wear a dress."

Amelia said, "I don't care if boys look at my underpants. How much will they pay me?"

"They're not paying you. They're just looking."

"Never mind. I'm wearing long pants."

"Me too," said Helene.

Mother said, "Thanks for the tape, Sonny Boy. Now I have to get it myself."

I said, "Sara, may I please speak to you downstairs?"

"Girls? Daddy and I have to go downstairs."

"Daddy?" said Helene. "Can we put the flowers in our hair?"

"Don't use the flowers on the kitchen table. They're for Aunt Mim."

Downstairs, I kissed Sara. "MIS rehired me for $65,000."

"What else?"

"Roger said they also hired you. He wants to see you on Fridays."

"They better let you leave early. When do you start?"

"In a month. But in three weeks I have to spend a week in Boca Raton, to learn C++, a new programming language.

Roger's going to pay for you and the girls. It won't be like Mel, because our hotel won't be as nice. We can go early, and see Disney World. I would also like to stop at Royal Palms. Let's see how Charles and Bruce are doing."

"You want to see Angie. Bring her dope. You might get lucky."

"Is it dope or coke? I forget."

"It's all dope to me. The people who do it are dopes. I will go wherever you want, if you let me handle the apartment and school. I'm spending the next two days at the school as an observer."

"Fine. Drop me at Barnes and Noble tomorrow. I'm also going to J&R. I want a laptop."

"Good. Get me a Powerbook with a nice case. I'm sure I'll find something to do with it."

Sara showed me her empty bottle of Scotch. "Be a good husband. Find us a drink upstairs. I want you to be calm."

I returned with two water glasses full of liquor.

Sara said, "First of all, I bought a different apartment. We own nine rooms on the corner of Riverside Drive and 103rd Street."

"How much?"

"625. I took a twenty year mortgage. Our monthly maintenance is $550. The garage is another hundred. We can afford it."

"I'm not worried. Tell me about the school."

"I'm not sure about this school. I didn't like Amelia's teacher. Her name is Anna. She's British, but she also teaches Japanese. I want our daughters to learn Spanish. Anna said they won't offer Spanish until the winter. One term of Japanese is a waste of time."

Sara paused for a sip. "Helene's teacher was worse. They're counting and doing A–B–C. She needs to be with older kids."

Sara chugged her drink. "Finish your drink. Come next to me."

Sara held my hand and stroked my head. "Our daughters need another tutor. Amelia was the tallest kid in her group. She should be in a modeling school. Helene should start art lessons or piano. We can't afford everything.

But I have an idea. I took the larger apartment for a reason. I want to put my mother in one of the bedrooms. Let her tutor the girls. Mom was a real teacher. She'll know what she's doing. We can all learn Spanish together."

I said Sara's least–favorite word, "But," before she said, "I never complain about your crazy mother. At least my mother's sane."

"Saner. How about if we give the school one more day? Can you please speak to the director tomorrow?"

"One more day. Go upstairs and get us two more drinks. Tell your mother to make dinner. Then get back here and remind me why I married you."

I was absorbed in a C++ book at noon, when Sara bellowed, "Get over here right now."

"What did I do? I bought you a beautiful laptop."

"Who cares. You should have listened to me. Talk to her."

Tears flowed down Amelia's cheeks. Sara said, "Show Daddy what they gave you at school."

It was a pamphlet titled "Have you seen these at home?" from "D.A.R.E." — "Drug Abuse Resistance Education."

Underneath the title was a name, "Officer Paul Zabarowski" and his telephone number. The pamphlet included photos of marijuana, pills and a glassine envelope.

Amelia said, "One boy told the officer that he saw something. He called another officer. The second officer took the boy out of the room, and the boy never came back. The first officer said he would find a new place for us to live if our parents went to jail."

"May I please see the paper?" said Helene.

Helene pointed to the photos. "I've seen this, and this, and this. I've seen everything. He didn't ask me. You won't have to go to jail, Daddy. You don't have to go either, Mommy. We can stay here with Uncle Ralph and Aunt Mim."

Amelia squeezed my hand. "I swear I didn't say anything. I only want to live with you and Mommy."

I held Amelia while she calmed down. Then I started to laugh. Amelia responded by punching me in the nose.

I held her fist until she said, "Why were you laughing?"

"I wonder what Mommy will say to Officer Zabarowski."

Sara said, "You don't know me."

"You only know her for ten minutes," said Helene.

Sara ignored her. "I'm going to get this guy. Oh boy, am I going to get him. This filthy home–wrecker will never know it's me. He's worse than a lawyer. Somebody has to stop him.

He's got no business interfering with other people's private lives. This school, an expensive private school, has no business inviting him. He won't be working around here when I'm through with him."

Mother, Ralph and Mim woke up and joined us. Sara faced them and smiled. "I'm friends with criminals. I meet them in emergency rooms."

"What kind of criminals? Are you bringing them here?" said Ralph.

"Police, Ralph. There's a fine line between cops and criminals. Like there's a fine line between medical Doctors and dope dealers.

I could open an office tomorrow, write prescriptions for dope and make plenty of money. I can write the same prescriptions for dope and trade them for favors with cops.

They all want Percodan. I'm going to make calls. Zabarowski should be an easy name to find."

Ralph held her arm. "What's going to happen to him?"

"Someone will find his car, tow it somewhere, but say he towed it somewhere else. It will take a month to find it.

It might get towed again the following day. The boys will come up with other stuff. Someone will find his supervisor and get him assigned somewhere else."

"What did he do?"

Sara released her arm. "Ask your nephew."

Only Mother was smiling when I finished. Mother said, "Why don't we take the girls out? Let's buy flowers and tape."

Before I could answer, Sara bellowed, "Get in here right now!"

"You've got some wife, Sonny. At least she's not boring."

Mim's palm smacked Ralph's cheek. "Am I still boring?"

"Sonny?" said Sara. "Get us two drinks and sit with me."

She took a sip and pointed to my glass. She waited for me to drink half.

"You're my husband, my one true love. I need you here with me."

"What can I do?"

"Sit there while I make two telephone calls."

"Hi Mom. We all need you now. I had to take Amelia and Helene out of their school. You're going to be their new tutor.

We bought a nine room apartment in our old neighborhood. You have your own bedroom. I've also got my mother–in–law, because my father–in–law died.

Tell Bob you're going to see Ted. Take your purse. Don't take anything else. Walk over to Ted's. We're spending three weeks in Florida before we move in. You're leaving right now. I'm calling Ted. He'll drive you to the airport."

Her mother must have said, "But." Sara bellowed, "You better leave now or you will never see your grandchildren again!"

A moment later, she said, "Good," and hung up.

Sara's bellow attracted Mother, Ralph and Mim. Mother asked, "What are you talking about?"

Sara said, "Not you. My mother," while she dialed.

"Hi Ted. Please help Mom meet me at the Jacksonville Beach Suites Hotel, in Florida. Mom is walking over to you. Drive her to the airport, and put her on a flight to Jacksonville. Please wait until she leaves. I don't want her changing her mind. Thank you."

"He saw her crossing the road. There's one more thing."

We watched Sara finish her drink.

"We've all been under a tremendous amount of stress. I'm a Doctor. Trust me. There is nothing worse than stress."

Sara handed me her empty glass. Ralph said, "When I'm under stress, I eat ice cream."

"Make me a small one, Sonny Boy," said Mother.

Sara waited until I gave everyone a drink. Our surprised daughters received cups of chocolate milk.

"We found a delightful hotel, the Jacksonville Beach Suites. It has beautiful rooms and five restaurants. You can even go bowling."

Mother said, "I won't wear anybody else's shoes."

"You can buy your own bowling shoes. I am sure they sell them at this hotel," said Sara.

Mother pulled a credit card from the pocket of her house dress. "I have $50,000 on this card. The broker sent it to me. I can pay for everything."

"My mother's coming. Do you mind paying for her?"

"No. I would like to meet her."

"I would also like to meet her," said Mim.

Ralph dismissed his wife with a wave. "Forget it. We're not going."

"You're going! We're leaving right now," said Sara. "A van is picking us up any minute. Listen to me and we won't have any problems."

"Why should he listen to you?" said Mother. "I'm paying for this."

"You're right," said Sara. "Ralph? Listen to your sister."

"You should have been listening to me all along, Ralphie. I know things."

Ralph said, "I don't know whether to have ice cream or another drink."

"Have another drink. Ice cream will make a mess in the car," said Mim.

We heard two short honks in front of the house.

Sara said, "Bring paper cups and a bottle. Get in the car right now."

Nobody gave orders better than Sara.

Living Anatomy Lesson

The Grandmothers shared a room for two days.

Sara's mother wanted to know who should hold the exalted title of "Grandma." Mother won.

Instead of answering, Mother excused herself and went into the bathroom. Sara's mother knocked on the bathroom door until she got disgusted and left. I entered their unlocked room and announced myself as "United Parcel Service."

Mother opened the bathroom door, and peeked outside. "I knew it was you. Did she leave? Do I have to go back in there?"

"She left. What were you doing in there?"

"I was thinking about things."

I was wondering if they were Good Things when Mim knocked.

"She got in a cab. I thought she was nice. I knew she wouldn't last," said Mim.

Mother added, "I knew too. But I made sure."

I asked our remaining Grandma, "When did you know? Why didn't you tell me?"

"You're my son, I thought you knew. How old are you now? Whew! I'm getting dizzy trying to remember. Mim, help me into bed. I'm stiff. I was sitting in the bathtub for an hour. Mim, why don't you stay here with me?"

Mim was silent while I stared at Mother's toothless grin. "We can make up a good excuse to tell Ralph why you can't stay with him tonight. Let's play cards and order food."

Mim stretched out on the vacant bed. "I sprained my ankle and I can't walk back to our room."

Mother waved from her prone position. "Why are you here, Sonny Boy? Go find something else to do."

Mim removed her shoes and the top cover of the bed. She adjusted the pillows to see Mother.

"Why are you still here? Go bother your wife."

"I'm not leaving until you tell me how you knew Sara's mother would leave."

"How could you not know?"

After grunts and grimaces, Mother sat up high enough to look at me. "She's not Jewish, you idiot. How could you go to a Yeshiva and not understand? I hope you still speak Hebrew. Otherwise, the whole thing was a waste of time and money."

"What does this have to do with Sara's mother leaving?"

"She's not Jewish."

"What else?"

"Nothing else. She's not used to being around Jews. I knew she wouldn't last."

Mother grinned at Mim. "Why don't you move in with us?"

I said the dreaded, "But," before Mother said, "Walk over here so I can look at you and Mim at the same time without turning my head."

I pulled over a chair and sat between their beds.

"What did they teach you about Jews in school? We are the chosen people. We can do whatever we want."

I was silent. "Mim, can you believe this? They didn't teach him anything in Yeshiva."

"Why are you asking me? I agree with you. They should all be fired. Your son learned everything from you."

"Thank you."

"You're welcome. I know you a long time."

I interrupted. "Have you ever seen her behave like this? I've never seen her so calm."

"Keep quiet Mim. It's none of his business."

"I'm your son. Why wouldn't you tell me anything?"

Mother tried to shrug. "Ask Mim after I'm dead."

"You can ask me anything after she's gone."

I faced both women. "What about Sara?"

Mother waved at Mim. "Please explain this. Sonny Boy thinks we have all day. He should have known this when he was born."

Mim got up and moved her nose next to mine. "She's a Doctor, you idiot."

Mother turned to Mim. "By the way, I don't mind if you call my son an idiot. He knows we're kidding. But I never should have sent him to that school. I should have tutored him at home. Why don't you move in with us? We can tutor the girls together."

A reflex made me utter "But."

"It doesn't matter what you say! You bought the apartment with our money. It's our apartment, not yours," said Mother.

I stammered, "I'm the father. I have to live there."

Mother smiled. "You can be replaced. I have plenty of money. Sara might like someone younger than you."

Mother turned to Mim, "I bet she has to explain everything to him."

Mim said, "You're right," before they busted up laughing.

I wanted a glass of whiskey while I waited for them to stop laughing. "Let's get this over with, once and for all. Aunt Mim, please be quiet."

"I called you an idiot. You can tell me to be quiet."

I tried to sit near Mother, but she pushed my hip away.

"You must be an idiot. Why would you sit on my bed after you sat on a filthy chair?"

"Mother, please stop calling me an idiot."

Mother waved. "I called your father an idiot all the time. He never complained. He was a much bigger idiot than you. He didn't even know I was calling him an idiot half the time, because I didn't use that word. You fooled me all these years. I thought you were smart. What don't you understand? I'm sorry. I'll try to be nicer."

I waved at Mother. "Why is it okay for Sara to be Christian, but not her mother?"

"Her mother was boring. Sara must get her brains from her father. I would like to meet him. Sara is a physician. She's different. She might be the smartest person I ever met. Your daughters are smart. You were smart to marry her."

"I'm smart now?"

"You were always smart. Get going. First, look through the peephole, and see who's knocking."

I ignored Mother's request and opened the door. It was Uncle Ralph, wearing a lime green cabana shirt and matching shorts.

"Is Mim here?" Ralph pushed me aside and walked to her.

"I dropped the remote control. Then I accidentally kicked it under the bed. I can't reach it. Put on your shoes, and get it for me. I've got to change the channel to see the closing stock prices. Hurry up. It starts in five minutes."

Ralph pointed to her stockinged feet. "Where are your shoes?"

Mim's answer was preceded by the sound of her right palm smacking Ralph's left cheek. "Is this all I'm good for? To crawl under a filthy bed in a hotel for you?"

Mother smiled at Ralph. "She's right. You're an idiot. Take my son with you. Close the door on your way out. Make sure it's locked. We don't want surprise visitors."

Mim turned to Mother. "I could use a surprise visitor. Let's have a drink at the bar in the lobby."

"I'll go, but I don't want anyone to know it's me. Let's stop in your room for one of Ralph's hats."

Ralph's face turned crimson as he waddled to Mother. "If you're going to my room, I mean our room with her, why won't she get my remote control?"

Mother stuck out her arm. She waited for Ralph to help her out of bed before she answered. "You're right. I'll buy a nicer hat downstairs. Get out of here. Take my son with you. We're leaving and locking our door."

"Our door? You're staying with her, Mim? What did I do?" asked Ralph.

Mim stood up and smiled at her husband. "If you don't know, I'm not going to tell you."

Ralph whined, "What do I tell our kids?"

"Tell them your sister and I became lesbians. We moved to Manhattan to meet more lesbians."

A stabbing pain pierced my chest. "What about me?"

Mother laughed. "You're a bigger idiot than my brother, if you believed her."

"You stopped calling me an idiot. What happened? Are you still taking your pills?"

"I'm taking my pills. You're a bigger idiot than usual today."

Mother covered her hand with a tissue before she pushed Ralph. "Let's go before you do anything else."

Ralph asked, "Why are you holding a tissue?"

Mother pointed to the door. "Because you've been sitting on the chairs around here. Thanks for reminding me."

Mother tried to put a bottle of rubbing alcohol in her house dress pocket. She handed it to Mim. "Put this in your purse so we can wipe the chairs before we sit down."

Mother walked around Ralph and into the hall. "Hurry up, Mim! I pressed the button."

"What are you worried about, Ralph? Your sister's paying for everything. Order ice cream," said Mim.

I tugged on Ralph's shirt before he could answer, but Mim tugged back. She said, "Take the car keys," and dropped them in his hand as she passed us.

"Will you please get the remote control for me?"

I found his remote control. He said, "Thanks. What got into them today?"

"Have dinner with us. Speak to Sara."

"At least she's not boring."

I almost put my hand on his shoulder. "Uncle Ralph, please be nice to Aunt Mim."

"Mim's not here. What's the difference?"

"Please let Sara explain it to you."

A sunburned Sara persuaded Ralph to go home. He was in a better mood while we waited for a cab to the airport.

"Where is your bag, Uncle Ralph?"

"Mim will get it. She left her stuff there too."

Mother was right. He was an idiot.

Sara was applying cortisone cream to our daughters when I returned. "I ordered a babysitter," she said. "It's your job to interview her. Make me a drink, and have one too."

Sara wiped her hands while I filled two paper cups with whiskey. She finished her cup in two sips. "I don't understand why you bought small cups. Bring us another one before the babysitter gets here. I have to get dressed."

Ivy the babysitter was young and petite. I introduced her to our daughters, "This is Ivy."

Ivy got down on one knee and tried to shake their hands. My sensible daughters took a step back. They said, "Hi Ivy," together.

"Girls, Mommy and I are going out for three or four hours. Ivy is going to be in charge while we're away."

Helene tapped my leg. "I don't think so."

"Helene is correct," said Amelia. "I am the Boss if Mommy's not here and you're not here. Ivy can stay here. But she's not the Boss."

Amelia folded her arms and stared at me, daring me to challenge her. Helene tapped Ivy's shoulder. "We don't mind if you stay. But you can't be the Boss."

I smiled at Ivy. She said, "But."

"You're not allowed to use that word," said Amelia.

Ivy got up and walked toward Amelia. Amelia extended her arm, to keep Ivy away. "But. B–U–T. Don't you know this word?"

Ivy said, "But," before Amelia tugged on her blouse.

"Can you read?"

Ivy nodded.

"Good. You can read us stories. Then we can order food and watch a movie. I get to pick the stories."

Helene raised her hand.

"Helene gets to pick the movie. I can order room service for you. Oh, I almost forgot. You have to read all the characters in different voices or Helene and I will punish you. Got it?"

Ivy sat on a chair with her knees pulled up to her chest and her face buried between them.

Amelia pulled down my ear and whispered, "Is she going to be all right?"

I nodded.

"Can I test her before you leave?"

As soon as I smiled, Amelia said, "Ivy, take off your shoes. You are not allowed to wear shoes in here. Then go wash your hands before you touch my book."

Sara was in a great mood. She appeared wearing jeans and a bright red t–shirt with "Stuff Happens," in large yellow letters.

A shoeless Ivy said, "Hello." Amelia punched her shoulder and pushed her into the bathroom. "No talking until you wash your hands. And don't say 'But' – especially while Mommy's here."

Sara approached Amelia. "You're not allowed to punch Ivy. She's not your sister."

Helene asked, "Why is she allowed to punch me?"

Sara patted Helene's head. "Because you punch her back."

An unwashed Ivy stared slack jawed at Amelia. Ivy asked Sara, "Is she really the Boss?"

"She's the Boss when I'm not here. Go wash your hands."

Helene misunderstood her confusion. "Daddy used to be the Boss sometimes. But not any more. He doesn't mind. Right, Daddy?"

"I don't mind if Amelia's the Boss."

"Wait there. I want to write this down. You have to sign it before you leave," said Amelia.

Amelia ran off. I whispered to Ivy, "Please wash your hands."

Ivy was sobbing in the bathroom when Amelia returned with a paper and pen. Sara said, "Can you hear her crying? She's not used to you. Go easy on her. Daddy will sign your note later. Let me talk to our babysitter before we leave."

We heard Sara bellow, "Pull yourself together!"

"Ivy had a crisis," said Helene.

Amelia grinned. "It is only her first crisis. She should have a new crisis every fifteen minutes."

"How about once an hour?"

"I think every half hour is better," said Helene.

I sighed. "Okay. Every half hour. Please stop if she starts crying."

"She better not cry for more than a half hour," said Amelia.

"No punching Ivy," I said.

Sara gave me a big hug and kiss in the elevator. "I love it when things work out. Where are we going?"

"Let's check on Mother, then go bowling."

Mim waved from a table in the nearly empty lobby bar. Mother sat in a portable wheelchair, wearing a Miami Dolphins cap and wraparound sunglasses. "I bought this in the gift shop, to sit in a clean chair. Mim doesn't mind pushing me."

"I never saw you wear a baseball cap, Mother."

Mother smiled. "It's a football cap. I never wore one before. I don't want anybody to recognize me."

"Is everything okay, Aunt Mim?"

Mim shrugged. "It's better since your mother gave the bartender $10 to lower the music. We're leaving soon. We haven't met anyone interesting."

Sara and I stopped in the bowling alley, but they were having a tournament. We played two games of pool on their coin operated table.

Sara worried about Ivy. We returned to our room with five slices of chocolate cheese cake and three cups of milk.

I froze, holding the food when I saw Ivy on the couch. Helene held a wet washcloth on Ivy's forehead. Our babysitter's jeans rested on a chair next to the air conditioner. A blanket covered the writing desk.

Amelia rushed toward us. "It was her fault. Mommy, please look at Ivy's head."

I caught myself staring at Ivy's white panties, with "Foxy Lady" in red script. Ivy tried to sit up. Sara pushed her down.

Ivy whispered, "Please don't hit me."

"Stop staring at her like an idiot, Sonny. Make her a drink and unpack the food," said Sara.

"Don't ever call me an idiot again!"

Sara imitated Steve Martin. "Well, excuse me."

"I better go," said Ivy. She started to get up.

Sara pushed her down. "You're not going anywhere. I'm a Doctor. Listen to me."

Helene patted Ivy's head. "Don't worry. Mommy is going to be a surgeon. She doesn't know everything, only some things. She will be careful."

Helene faced Sara. "Mommy, should I get towels? Is there going to be lots of blood when you operate?"

I brought a paper cup of Scotch and a box of tissues to a whimpering Ivy.

"Drink it, Ivy. Ignore my husband. He's seen plenty of women," said Sara.

Ivy drank enough to calm down. "Give me your blouse," said Sara. "Girls, why is there blood on her pillow?"

Amelia held her hands behind her back. "I only hit her a few times. I used my new flashlight. Grandma bought us flashlights at the gift shop. We can read while you think we're sleeping."

Sara kneeled to her level and hugged her. "Darling, you don't need a flashlight. I can leave the light on. Can you please show me your flashlight?"

"Helene, please help me." They went to the closet and returned with the longest flashlight I ever saw.

Ivy pulled her knees back to her chest. Sara smiled disarmingly, although the unbroken lens was streaked with blood. I retrieved a bottle of rubbing alcohol to disinfect the flashlight. Helene and Amelia stood together, holding hands behind their backs.

Sara held the giant flashlight and shined it on the wall. "Did Grandma say why she bought you this flashlight?"

"Grandma said I needed the biggest flashlight to see better. She told us we could go blind if we looked at the light for a long time. Is this true?"

I opened the flashlight. I showed Sara eight batteries before she said, "Grandma is correct. But you would get a terrible headache. You would stop before you went blind."

Helene handed Sara a portable reading lamp. This lamp used a single penlight battery, and clipped on a book. Sara tried it and returned it to her. "Why didn't you get one like this, Amelia?"

Amelia pouted. "I'm the big sister. Whatever I get should be bigger than Helene's."

"Never mind. You're getting the same light as Helene. I'm not leaving the light on. I lied. Use your flashlights. I want Helene to tell me what happened."

"Amelia said we had to punish her. We knew she wasn't smart, after we gave her *Snow White* to read. Amelia told her to read all the parts in different voices. She didn't do a good job." Helene imitated Sara, looking down and shaking her head.

Sara asked Amelia, "You punished her because you didn't like her voices?"

Amelia crossed her arms. "Mommy, she's a professional babysitter. This is an expensive hotel. You have to pay her lots of money. I know she's not smart. I wouldn't have punished her if she couldn't teach me Japanese. She probably doesn't even know Math."

Helene tapped Amelia's hand. "I know Math."

"Of course you know Math, Helene. You're smart. She's stupid."

Ivy raised her right hand. Sara said, "Yes?"

"I got a 92 on my Math final. Why does everybody think I'm stupid?"

Amelia and Helene giggled.

"It's not nice to make fun of stupid people," said Sara.

Ivy said, "But."

Amelia pushed Ivy's shoulder. "You're not allowed to say that word when our family is here."

Amelia turned to Sara. "I didn't hit her. I pushed her. You didn't say anything about pushing."

"From now on, pushing is the same as hitting. You're only allowed to push each other."

"You let them hit each other?" said Ivy.

"Why not? They can hit back."

Ivy said, "But."

Sara pointed to Ivy. "Don't you ever tell me how to raise my daughters again!"

Ivy urinated on the couch, and tried to stand. Sara grabbed Ivy's ankles and pushed her back into her puddle. Sara stroked Ivy's head until her teeth stopped chattering.

Ivy tried to sit up. Sara pushed her down. "Relax. Are you okay?"

Amelia and Helene vanished. I felt Sara's bellow. "Get back here!"

Amelia and Helene kept their heads down.

"Look at me. You have one minute to explain how this happened. And I lied. I don't mind if you make fun of stupid people. They deserve it."

"Are you a medical Doctor?" said Ivy.

Sara pointed to a tan leather carry–on bag, "Do you see my bag?"

Sara waited for Ivy to nod.

"I have drugs in this bag to paralyze you. I also have drugs to kill you. It would be more fun for my husband if I paralyzed you."

Sara lowered her voice. "If you ever tell me how to raise my daughters again, I will tell my husband to hold you down and I will kill you in front of our daughters. It would be a good lesson for them."

Ivy looked at me. "Would you help her kill me?"

Amelia tapped my hip. "You're not allowed to answer. Ivy, he's not a Boss anymore. Daddy has to do whatever Mommy says. He has to do everything I say if Mommy's not here."

"I'm the Boss if Mommy and Amelia go out together," said Helene. "Then Daddy has to do whatever I say."

Ivy sat up, revealing a red stain on the pillow. Ivy asked Sara, "Would you really do that?"

Sara giggled. "Why don't you tell me how to raise my daughters again? Find out for yourself."

"What would you do?"

"We would buy a saw and a meat grinder, to flush everything but your bones down the toilet. I would also buy knives, to give my daughters an anatomy lesson."

Sara closed her eyes and laughed.

"What's funny about killing me?"

"It's not your fault. If I paralyzed you, I could give my daughters a living human anatomy lesson. I may never have another perfect chance like this, with someone I never met."

Ivy gasped. Helene tapped on Sara's shoulder until she turned. "Why would you want to do that to Ivy?"

Sara stroked Helene's head. "Darling, I love studying the human body. We only had dead bodies in medical school. Live bodies are more interesting. I became a surgeon to look inside living bodies."

Helene stroked Sara's cheek. "Mommy, can we please look inside Ivy?"

Ivy gasped and went flat. She closed her eyes, crossed her ankles, and covered her crotch with her hands. Ivy ignored the wet blanket on the floor next to the couch.

"Why are you forgetting me?" Amelia waved at Sara. "I would like to see this too. Will I be able to use the toilet while you are flushing Ivy? Will it take a long time?"

Sara ignored Amelia. She leaned next to Ivy and bellowed, "Boo!"

Ivy's teeth chattered.

Sara stroked Ivy's head. She purred, "You're going to be fine. It's hard to stop playing with you. I'll stop now. Relax."

Sara bellowed, "Girls! Get over here!"

Sara pointed to the beleaguered babysitter. "I want both of you to apologize to Ivy. Then I want to hear what happened."

Helene frowned. "Mommy, are you going to punish me?"

Sara smiled. "Have I ever punished you?"

"No."

"Why would I punish you now?"

"You never punished them?" said Ivy.

Sara stuck their noses together. "I'm going to pretend I didn't hear you. I don't want to kill you now. The more I think about it, it's going to make a big mess. You have to plan ahead for something like this."

Sara waved at me. "Did you hear me? We should plan ahead if we ever decide to carve someone up."

"We think alike. I've been thinking about supplies."

Sara told Ivy, "I married him because he's smart. He's also good in bed."

Helene asked, "Why are you good in bed, Daddy?"

"Mommy likes the way I read *Snow White*."

Amelia pushed her sister. "That's not what Mommy means. She's talking about sex. Grandma calls it the 'whosis' and 'whatsis'."

Amelia tapped on Sara's hip. "Mommy, if you're not going to kill Ivy, can we please watch Daddy having sex with her?"

Ivy gasped.

Sara smiled at me. "She's going to make me do it. You better start making a list."

Ivy whispered, "May I please have the blanket back?"

Amelia picked it up. "Yuck. It's wet," she said. Amelia dropped the wet blanket on Ivy.

Helene punched Ivy in the shoulder while she was unfolding the blanket. "You should have thanked Amelia for giving you the blanket."

Ivy studied Helene. "Are you a midget? Are you really a little kid?"

"I don't feel like answering your question right now."

"Wait. Did your mother teach you that?"

Helene shook her head. "No. Grandma taught me that."

Amelia pointed to me. "His mother," she said.

Ivy asked me, "Did your mother teach you that?"

"I don't remember. My mother is staying in this hotel. I can bring her over. Mother wanted a girl. She could adopt you. Want me to call her?"

"Will Grandma kill Ivy if she comes here? It doesn't look like Mommy's going to do it. I would like to eat soon," said Amelia.

"You never know what his mother will do," said Sara.

Ivy drooled. Sara told Helene, "We're out of tissues. Please bring me a roll of toilet paper."

Ivy smiled at Sara. "You don't have to keep wiping me. I can put on my wet clothes and leave."

Sara pinched Ivy's cheek.

"See what happens if you try to leave. I don't have to do anything. It might be fun to watch my husband hold you down while my daughters take turns hitting you with a flashlight."

"I did that before. Do I have to do it again? Can't we watch Daddy and Ivy have sex? Grandma bought us cameras. I would rather take pictures of Daddy having sex," said Amelia.

"Never mind. Amelia, please explain what happened to Ivy," said Sara.

"Please don't hurt me again. I won't try to leave," said Ivy.

Sara faced Amelia. "What happened?"

"First we put a blanket over the desk, to make a little house. Ivy read *Snow White* to us under the blanket. She used my big flashlight to see the book. But she did a bad job.

Ivy did not behave like a professional babysitter. She knew she would be punished. Helene and I punched her in the arm for her first two mistakes. Then we fooled her."

Sara asked, "How did you fool her?"

Ivy said, "She…she…"

Sara acknowledged her. "It's not your turn yet."

Ivy said, "Thank you," and relaxed.

Amelia continued. "I told her the big flashlight was giving me a headache and she had to use the smaller one."

Sara interrupted. "Did you have a headache?"

"Maybe a little one."

"Did you know you can get a headache when you don't have enough air to breathe?"

"No, Mommy."

"The next time you put three people under a blanket, leave one side open. What happened after Ivy used Helene's flashlight?"

"She made mistakes. She couldn't see me, so I hit her head with the flashlight. Ivy said, 'Ouch,' but I didn't think she was punished enough. I hit her again. Helene helped me. We hit her one or two more times."

"Please don't punish me. Amelia was my Boss. I had to help her. I had no choice," said Helene.

Sara patted Helene's head. "Don't worry. Nobody's getting punished except Ivy." Sara smiled at Ivy. "I don't punish my children. I'm not related to you."

Sara hugged Helene. "Please tell me how she got the bump in front of her head. And how did her pants get wet?"

"I'm sorry. Ivy hurt my ears with her screaming, after we hit her with Amelia's flashlight. I pushed her away. Ivy hit her head on the front of the desk when she tried to get up," said Helene. "It was an accident, Mommy. It wasn't more punishment. Ivy fell asleep after she hit her head. Amelia and I watched cartoons, until she woke up."

Sara asked, "How did her pants get wet?"

Ivy uttered a syllable. Sara held up her hand, "It's not your turn."

Ivy smiled. "Thank you, Sara."

"I didn't give you permission to speak, and I didn't give you permission to use my first name."

"Sonny, bring us two drinks," said Sara.

Ivy waved. I brought Ivy a paper cup. Sara and I watched her swallow two ounces of whiskey.

Sara looked at Ivy. "You're next, Ivy. Helene, please finish. I'm hungry. How did Ivy's pants get wet after she woke up?"

"It was an accident. Ivy said she was too tired to read after she woke up. I told her to drink your special coffee."

Sara always packed a two–cup electric pot to boil water, plus filters and her current favorite coffee.

"Ivy didn't know how to use the pot. She spilled hot water on her leg. Ivy said, 'Ow!' I told her to take her pants off. Helene gave her a piece of ice and put her pants by the air conditioner to dry faster."

"Is it my turn?" asked Ivy.

Sara shrugged. "Go ahead."

Ivy removed her cover and pushed it off the bed. Amelia said, "Hey! I gave that to you."

Ivy motioned for me to come closer. "I like you. You're nicer than your wife. Why did you marry her?"

"To make two genius daughters."

Ivy asked Sara, "Is he really as smart as you?"

Sara remembered something and laughed. "Sometimes he's smarter."

I said, "Thank you," and enjoyed the rest of my drink.

"I'm sorry I caused all this trouble. You're right. I was stupid. I should never have let two little kids hurt me. I've been working here for six months. I don't understand what happened today," said Ivy.

"I'll explain one thing, even though you probably won't remember it later," said Sara.

She pointed to our daughters. "They're not kids or midgets. They're geniuses. You underestimated them. Helene, please bring me my bag. Amelia get over here."

Sara took her bag. "Give Ivy a kiss. Tell her you're sorry again."

Amelia distracted Ivy while Sara filled a syringe and placed it on her bag, out of Ivy's sight. She picked up Ivy's blouse and held it behind her back with her right hand. Sara smiled at Ivy, before the love of my life and I went into action.

I sat on Ivy's legs. I pinned her scrawny arms while Sara gagged her with her blouse. Sara held her face down with her left hand and showed Ivy the syringe with her right.

"Relax. I'm not going to kill you. I'm going to put you to sleep. You won't remember anything when you wake up," said Sara.

"We didn't mind having you as our babysitter. You can come back after you practice reading *Snow White*. If you don't have *Snow White* at home, you can borrow it from the library," said Helene.

"When are you coming back?" said Amelia. "I want to start making a list of everything we need from the gift shop to be ready for you."

Sara dropped Ivy's blouse, grabbed Amelia's arm, and pulled her over. "She's not coming back. You never saw her. Do you understand?"

Amelia nodded and tugged her arm free.

Sara pointed to Helene. "If you see her in the hotel, don't say 'Hello.' You don't know her. None of this happened. Do you understand?"

"I understand," said Helene.

"We understand. Does Daddy understand?" said Amelia.

Sara cut me off with a wave. "You better keep quiet or I'll make Daddy a Boss again."

"I wish you elected him Boss before I got here," said Ivy.

"Don't you remember what I told you? You're not allowed to tell me how to raise my daughters. You're not allowed to give me advice about anything. You caused this trouble by letting two little girls take advantage of you. Get over here girls."

Our angelic daughters smiled at Ivy.

Ivy stared at the girls.

"You're a babysitter. Have you ever seen two kids their age, with half of their intelligence? Or better manners? Nobody has better manners than my kids. Our kids. My husband helps. He's a good husband. Sorry, Amelia. I'm making him a Boss again."

"Why?"

"Helene's the next Boss, ahead of you."

"That's not fair."

"Fair? Nothing's fair. The only reason I can take care of Ivy, and you don't have to go to reform school, is because I'm a Doctor. Ivy could not be a Doctor. Would you like to be a medical Doctor, Ivy?"

"Oh, no. I want to be a nurse. My mother is a nurse."

The room filled with laughter until Ivy said, "What's wrong with being a nurse?"

Amelia patted Ivy's head. "Don't be sad."

"Why?"

"My mother said I'm smarter than any nurse. I'm smarter than your mother."

"Me too. Mommy, am I smarter than her mother?" said Helene.

Sara sighed. "This is turning into an ordeal. You might as well bring a bottle in here. I need a drink. Wait until Daddy brings me another drink."

Sara patted Ivy's head. "No more for you. I want you to wake up. Don't you want to wake up? I can kill you if don't want to wake up."

Sara took a long sip of her drink. "Do you ever feel like killing yourself? Don't worry, I won't kill you. I want to know. Do you ever get depressed?"

"Only once. I failed my French midterm last year. I think my boyfriend was seeing somebody else, and…"

Amelia tapped Ivy's shoulder. "If you have a boyfriend, you must tell us about him."

Helene shoved Amelia aside. "Please tell us his name. You must begin by telling us his name."

"Well, I don't have a boyfriend now. I've seen this one guy three times and…"

Sara covered Ivy's mouth with her hand. "Stop. I don't want to spend all night on this. I would love to be a shrink, but I don't want you to be my first patient.

I want to ask my husband a question. I'll let you ask a question, then I'll finish this. I'm hungry."

Sara faced me. "Am I slipping? Have I lost control? I enjoy talking to Ivy. Am I getting soft?"

"You're not getting soft. Our daughters would enjoy watching you get mean. They might think about it the next time they want to torture a babysitter."

Sara smiled. "Thank you."

Amelia tapped Sara's shoulder. "Will you please tell us at least one day before we have another babysitter? I want to make sure we are more prepared next time."

Amelia whispered in Sara's ear. "Can we do it Mommy? Please?"

"No."

"Ha! You finally said 'No.' What did she want to do?" said Ivy.

"She cut the wire off the lamp. She wanted to plug it in and put it between your legs to see what happens."

Ivy gasped. "Why would she want to hurt me?"

Helene put her hand on Ivy's mouth. "Be quiet. Mommy, can I please hold the wire first?"

Amelia ran two steps and shoved Helene out of the way. "It was my idea. Helene should only be allowed to hold the wire after I'm done. Unless you and Daddy want to hold it."

"Time out," said Sara. "I am the Boss. We are not going to electrocute Ivy."

"If we're not going to do it, at least tell me what would happen," said Amelia.

"I don't think it would do much. Ivy's had enough. You'll have to try it on somebody else."

"Thank you," said Ivy.

"Don't thank me, thank my mother," said Amelia. "If you want to thank me for something, be glad Helene and I didn't do it to you while you were sleeping."

"She wasn't sleeping," said Sara. "Ivy was unconscious."

"I'm sorry," said Amelia.

"Babysitters will come here to see if they can live until Mommy and Daddy come home. Every babysitter will know us," said Helene.

"We don't want every babysitter to know us. It has to be a secret, Helene. If somebody gets mad they could make us go to school. The only person who knows is Ivy. Oh Mommy! I wish you would kill her. Please?"

"I'm not going to kill Ivy. She's not going to remember anything."

Sara emptied the rest of the bottle into her glass. She toasted me and took a sip. "Okay Ivy, ask your question."

"Have your daughters done this to other babysitters?"

"We never had a complaint about their behavior. I don't think they need a babysitter. None of this would have happened if we left them alone for a couple of hours," said Sara.

Helene tapped Sara's arm. "Please don't say that. I think it would be more fun if we could have a new babysitter every night. Mommy can we..." Helene whispered in Sara's ear.

"We're never having another babysitter!"

"Mommy, it was educational. You said I could do anything if it was educational."

"You're not allowed to hurt more people."

Ivy whispered, "What did she want to do?"

"You're lucky we came home early. Her Grandmother bought her a watch. She wanted to tie a plastic bag around your head and use her new watch to measure the time it took for you to pass out and wake up."

Ivy fainted. Sara gave her an injection.

"I gave her Versed," said Sara. "I wouldn't let them give it to you before your operation because one of its side effects is amnesia. Ivy probably won't remember anything from the past two weeks. Please go down the hall. Get me a bunch of towels from a maid's cart and something to eat from the machine. I'll figure out what to do with her."

I returned with armloads of towels, three boxes of tissues and peanut butter crackers. Sara was checking Ivy's pulse. "She's fine. Remember what you told me before you moved in?"

"You were the most intelligent person in the world."

"Correct. You said I was the most intelligent person you will ever meet. Girls, are you listening?"

"Daddy said you were the smartest person," said Helene.

Sara asked, "Amelia, did you hear me?"

"Yes, Mommy."

"You're all lucky. We could go to jail for this," said Sara.

I laughed. "I didn't do anything."

Sara giggled. "Are you kidding? I am a Doctor. Judges and police consider me an expert. I could blame the whole thing on you."

"Mommy? If Daddy went to jail, would they let him be the Boss? Maybe not the big Boss, but one of the bosses?" said Helene.

"Darling, if Daddy went to jail he'd be somebody's wife. They like them tall and thin."

"Daddy, you're going to have to wear a dress in jail," said Amelia.

"Daddy, I don't mind. You can still be my Daddy. I will visit you in jail," said Helene.

"Girls, if something happened, I would tell the police that Daddy wasn't here."

"Why, Mommy?" said Helene.

Sara kissed me. "Because one of us in jail is enough. I know he would take good care of you if something happened to me. I married him because I knew he would be the best father in the world."

I kissed Sara. "Thank you."

"Mommy?" said Amelia. "If you're not killing Ivy, can you please cut her open? I want to look inside her."

Sara patted Amelia's head. "I'm not cutting Ivy open. Forget it."

"Can we please have one more babysitter?" said Helene.

Sara grabbed both girls and held their wrists. "I'm going to say this once. You are never, I repeat never, having another babysitter. If I decide to kill someone, to have a living anatomy lesson, it will be a surprise."

Sara released the girls and looked at me. "It's a little sick. Maybe I can find a nurse who lives alone. I could get addicted to it. If I did it all the time, I might get sloppy and be caught."

"Mommy, if you're not going to kill Ivy, can we please watch Daddy have sex with her? Please Mommy! How long does it take? Please Mommy, I want to see this," said Amelia.

Sara pulled over a chair and sat. "What the heck. I'm drunk. It would be fun to watch. You girls are old enough to watch sex. Go ahead. I'll get you tested later. I'll kill both of you if you catch anything."

"I'm sorry, Daddy," said Helene. "I'm sorry, but I want to see this. So I'll say 'Goodbye' now. I'm sure Mommy will kill you, even if you don't get sick."

Sara grinned. "I'm not sure. It doesn't matter because Daddy's too scared to do this. A man can't have sex if he's scared, only a woman can. It's called 'rape' and a different subject."

"I know rape is bad," said Amelia.

Helene patted my shoulder. "It's not rape because Ivy told me she wanted to have sex with you. It doesn't matter if she's sleeping. Please start now. I'm getting hungry. Otherwise, please call room service and let's eat first."

"Why didn't she tell me? I was the Boss," said Amelia.

I sighed. "Never mind. I'll do it now." I wiggled my hips, opened the button on my pants, and wiggled again.

Amelia pleaded, "Please hurry."

Sara patted her head. "Don't rush him. Women like it better when a man takes a long time."

"I better take a nap until something happens. Amelia, please wake me up when Daddy is having sex with Ivy," said Helene.

Amelia pushed Helene. "I never saw it before. Why would you ask me?"

"I'm sorry. Daddy, can you please stop for a minute, and wake me when you get to the good part?"

"Never mind. I'm not going to do it. It's not a good idea."

"I knew it. I knew you would chicken out," said Amelia.

"It's okay, Daddy. I'm glad you didn't have sex. I think Mommy was trying to trick you. I didn't want you to die. I love you Daddy," said Helene.

"Why would you say that? It could be years before we get to see this," said Amelia. "I want to see it now. Go get your camera. Take a picture of Daddy if you think you're going to miss him. Hurry up!"

"I'm not getting my camera. It won't be the same to have a picture."

Sara moaned. "Why does everybody want me to kill her? Look at her. She is peaceful. Why should I kill her?"

Amelia shook her head. "You're not fooling anyone, Mommy. We all know you want to kill her. Right Helene? Right Daddy?"

"It doesn't matter what Mommy wants. She's not going to kill her. We will see Ivy in the lobby tomorrow and say, 'Hi Ivy.' And she will be alive," said Helene.

I grabbed a wrist from each girl until they looked at me.

"Do you want Mommy to kill somebody else someday?"

The girls cheered, "Yay!"

"It's never going to happen if you talk to Ivy, or tell anyone what happened here. You can't tell anyone. Not even Grandma and Aunt Mim. Do you understand me?"

Both girls nodded.

"Okay. This will be a test. If you don't tell anyone for a whole year, Mommy will kill someone next year."

"I'll kill someone next year," said Sara. "We can't do it like this. We need a plan. It's not worth going to jail to have a little fun. It's not personal. I don't have to hate someone to kill them.

If someone bothers you, tell Daddy and me. We'll get rid of them for you. Don't forget, your father is smart or I wouldn't have married him. If either of you make a mistake and marry the wrong person, Daddy and I will kill them for you. Don't worry about it."

"Mommy? Can I marry the wrong person on purpose, to watch you kill him? Excuse me, I want to watch you and Daddy kill him. I want to see Daddy kill someone," said Helene.

Amelia patted Helene's head. "We all want to see Daddy kill someone. But you shouldn't marry a stupid person to see this. It's not worth it."

Sara sobbed. "She's right. My little girl is wise beyond her years."

Amelia beamed. "See Helene? I was right. I've never been married. I guessed."

Helene punched Amelia's arm. "Big deal."

"Why did you punch me? I was being nice to you. Now apologize, before I tell Mommy the Boss to tell Daddy to punch you. He can hit harder than me. Mommy, can you please tell Daddy to punch Helene for me?"

Sara laughed. "I will kill Daddy if he ever punches either of you."

"Would you still kill Daddy if he had sex fast, and you didn't see it? Mommy can you please go to the bathroom and stay there until Daddy's finished sexing Ivy?" said Helene.

Amelia shoved Helene harder than usual. "Sexing is not a word. I'll bet you a hundred dollars. It is not in the dictionary."

"Two hundred. Let's bet two hundred, Amelia."

I asked, "Where did you get all that money?"

"Grandma gave it to us for an emergency," said Helene.

Sara muttered, "Figures," and took a sip.

"Helene, get your money and meet me right here."

Both girls ran away. Sara and I watched each other sip our drinks. I said, "It will be over soon. Don't worry."

"I've never worried about anything. I'm becoming too nice. Maybe I'm getting old."

Helene met Amelia between the couch and desk, behind Ivy's head. Sara said, "Let me see that money."

Amelia wiggled the bills behind Ivy's head. "You'll have to come here if you want to see our money."

A grim Sara looked at me. "I've lost control. What happened to me?"

Sara spilled her drink reaching over Ivy for the bills. I heard a loud buzz because Amelia plugged in the lamp cord, and placed it under the bills. Sara said, "Oh." She collapsed on the couch, next to Ivy.

I looked into Sara's eyes as I cradled her head and smelled her burned hair. Sara's eyes lost focus as she moved her lips. I cursed myself for avoiding the CPR course she recommended. A person becomes brain dead in four minutes.

Sara would not want to be a vegetable. She had a living will with an explicit "do not resuscitate" order. I hugged Amelia. "Why did you do this?"

Amelia shook herself free. "Mommy said to try it on someone else. She said nothing would happen. Mommy was always right about everything until now. How was I supposed to know she would make a mistake?"

Helene patted my shoulder. "She's right. Amelia would never kill Mommy on purpose."

Amelia hugged me. "I'm sorry, Daddy. I know you loved Mommy. What do we do now? You better make sure I don't get sent away to a school. You know it was an accident. A judge or a nurse might not believe me."

I kissed the top of Amelia's head. "I know it was an accident."

Helene tapped my hip. "What do we do now, Daddy?"

"I have an idea. Amelia, give me the money."

"Here. I don't even like touching it. Grandma gave us more if you need it."

I placed the live wire near Ivy. I dried the bills and brushed my teeth before we left. "Nobody hit Ivy. She started crying, all by herself. We left Mommy to talk to her. If anybody asks you anything, pretend to be stupid. Say, 'I don't know' or 'I am not sure.' This is important. Are you both ready?"

The girls nodded. I led them, one in each hand, to the front desk. I asked an employee, "Is there a security office? We're having a problem with our babysitter."

Security was in the basement. Officer Richard Dickens sat behind a desk, dressed in a light blue uniform. He was playing Solitaire. I started to laugh, thinking, "Dick Dickens, the Dick,' until Amelia kicked me. My daughters smiled like they were auditioning for a movie.

Officer Dickens said, "Well, what have we here?"

"Excuse me. We're in 612. My wife and I left our daughters with a babysitter. The babysitter was crying, and acting weird when we returned. I think she's drunk. The room is a mess. My wife is talking to her. Would you mind coming up for a minute and getting rid of the babysitter for us?"

"Thanks for giving me something to do. What's this babysitter's name?"

"Ivy. Do you know her?"

"I don't know her. Let's see what she did. I'll put her in a cab if she's drunk. The manager can talk to her tomorrow."

We heard Ivy snoring as we opened the door. I said, "Sara?"

Helene stood next to Sara. "She can't answer, Daddy. She's dead. Ivy killed her."

Dick walked up to the couch. "Stand back." He looked sick. I led him to a chair. "Take it easy. One death is enough."

Dick lit a cigarette. "Do you mind if I smoke?"

I handed him an ashtray, and sat on the floor next to his chair.

"Thanks. I haven't had a murder in a long time. Don't worry. You're a nice fellow with two nice kids. If you killed her, she deserved to die."

"He didn't kill her. I did," said Amelia.

"I didn't hear you."

I handed Dick $400. "Please take this and buy a hearing aid."

"Thanks. I haven't had a bribe in a long time." Dick looked around. "I'll handle everything. Do you mind if I have a drink?"

I returned with two water glasses full of whiskey. Dick drank half of his drink. He said, "You've got great kids. I wish one of my kids would kill my wife for me. She's always spending money."

"We would like to help you," said Helene.

Dick chuckled and slapped his knee. "How can a little kid help me?"

Amelia punched his shoulder. "We're not little kids. We don't have to kill your wife. She's not bothering us. We were trying to do you a favor."

"What do I have to do?"

"Tell your wife she can make $100 for being our babysitter tomorrow."

"That's it?"

"Give her the number of our room."

"We can't stay in this room," said Amelia. "We will have to give him our new room number. I want to watch Daddy have sex with her, before he cuts her up into little pieces and flushes her down the toilet."

"I never said I would do this."

"You're not the Boss," said Amelia.

"Daddy, I want to cut her up too." said Helene.

Dick asked, "What about me?"

Helene waved at him. "We didn't invite you."

Dick was quiet until he finished his drink. "Say, if this works out, could you kill my mother–in–law? Can you help me out with her?"

"Stop acting like an idiot. We can only kill one person at a time," said Amelia.

Helene waved at her. "He's not an idiot. He's helping us. I'll be right back."

Helene returned with her camera. "Officer Dickens, please get closer to Ivy. I want to take a picture of everybody."

Dick said, "But…"

"You better do whatever we tell you, or we'll say you killed Mommy because she caught you having sex with Ivy," said Amelia.

Dick chuckled. "You can't do that."

"Then we will tell the police you asked Daddy to kill your wife and her mother. Daddy will tell them everything," said Helene.

I covered my face and cried until Helene tapped on my shoulder. "I know you miss Mommy. We all miss Mommy. Amelia didn't kill her on purpose."

"Be quiet. Don't be nice to Daddy. He'll expect us to be nice to him all the time," said Amelia.

"Mommy died. He misses her."

"I know. Don't you remember how she died?"

Helene shook her head. "I can't remember how Mommy died right now."

"You're a lot smarter than you look," said Amelia.

"What do you mean?"

"We'll talk about it later, Helene. Don't worry, Officer Dickens. We won't be able to remember what happened to your wife."

Amelia tapped my shoulder and whispered, "Go to the gift shop. Get a small notebook and a book for our anatomy lesson." She raised her voice, "and Twister for our party with Officer Dickens's wife."

A revived Dick leaned forward. "You're going to kill my wife playing Twister?" He shook his head muttering, "Twister."

Helene tapped his shoulder. "We'll have a nice time with your wife for one hour. Then we'll get tired of her. The party will be over. Only she won't be able to leave." Helene showed Dick her evil grin.

"Be quiet Helene. Don't give away our secrets," said Amelia.

I waved at Amelia. "We never had secrets while Mommy was alive."

"Be quiet, Daddy. We have new rules now. Everyone thinks we're little kids. Little kids can get away with anything."

Amelia sighed. "Daddy may have to kill the bigger people for us."

"I will?"

"You don't have to rush," said Dick.

Amelia and Helene said, "Be quiet!"

Dick froze.

"See how well we work together? Let's not fight. We must work together. Can we scream loud enough to make Officer Dickens wet his pants?" said Amelia.

"See here. I'm in charge," said Officer Dickens.

Amelia waved. "The only thing you're good for is bringing us another person to kill."

Helene punched Dick's shoulder. "Yeah! We want another person to kill."

"You shouldn't hit him. You should be nice to him," said Amelia.

Helene smiled and patted his shoulder. "I'm sorry. Would you like to have another drink?"

Dick smiled and stood up. "Well thank you, little girl. I could use another drink. We can't schmooze too long. There are two bodies on the couch. One of them better wake up before the end of my shift. I'm only working for another hour."

Helene pointed to his chair. "Why are you standing up? Amelia and I did not give you permission to stand. Please sit down or I will ask Daddy to beat you up."

I smiled my evilest grin at Dick. He looked at me. "Is it okay if I go to the bathroom?"

Helene waved. "Daddy is not the Boss. You can go. Come right back and sit in your chair."

Ivy moaned and stirred. "Hurry up or we will make you have sex with her," said Amelia.

"I don't mind. I won't be able to do anything, if you don't let me go to the bathroom," said Detective Dickens.

Helene said, "What are you waiting for?"

"Not so loud. We don't want to wake Ivy up until Officer Dickens is ready," said Amelia.

The girls walked over to me while Dick was in the bathroom.

"It's not nice for Officer Dickens to have sex with Ivy. It's 'rape.' He is not a nice man. We don't know his wife. She might be nice. We can't believe him. Let's kill him. Everybody who wants to kill Officer Dickens, please raise your hands," said Amelia.

My daughters raised their hands. I wondered if Sara would have helped them.

"Daddy, you should have raised your hand. Two against one – we kill him. Sorry Daddy, you lose. We have to do this fast. Let's get the flashlight. Daddy, it's better if you don't know what we're going to do. Mommy liked surprises and I hope you do too. This is going to be fun. Come Helene."

Helene said, "Daddy, you are not allowed to get up, unless we miss, and you have to finish the killing job."

Amelia pulled her arm, "Don't waste time talking to Daddy."

I took a sip of calming whiskey. Dick flushed the toilet. He opened the door without washing his hands.

I handed Dick a refreshed drink. "I'm sorry. I got a little worked up before."

"Sorry? You gave me four hundred dollars. Now I'm going to get laid for the first time in three years. Oh boy! Am I glad I met you and your daughters. Let me sit down and have a drink. Then I'll be ready for Ivy. I'll get overtime doing the paperwork. This is a great day. Don't be sorry for anything."

"I'm really sorry."

"Don't be ashamed. Everyone reacts to death differently."

I stared at my drink until I heard Dick say, "What the…" He fell from the chair on his side. Amelia and Helene stood over him. Dick started to say "But" before the girls swung the flashlight together at his forehead.

They hit him five times, until blood ran out of his nose. I kneeled down. Dick was breathing. I did not feel like touching him.

I used a pair of surgical gloves from Sara's bag to remove $400 from Dick's wallet. I had no idea if he would remember anything. Dick settled it when he made a noise. I smashed his forehead with the flashlight until I ran out of breath.

My daughters were smiling.

Amelia hugged my leg. "I'm glad you joined our murder gang. You hit him hard. I liked watching you."

"I liked watching you Daddy," said Helene. She hugged my other leg. "Thank you for killing him. He was going to rape Ivy. Poor Ivy."

I placed the flashlight on Ivy's side and wrapped her sleeping hand around it. I wrestled a dead Dick, until I was able to pull down his pants and underpants. He had a giant erection. I put the gloves back in Sara's bag.

"He has a big penis," said Amelia.

"It's called an erection. He was ready to have sex with Ivy. I'm glad we killed him. Ivy's going to be in enough trouble."

Helene asked, "Daddy? Can we please cut off his penis, and save it in a plastic bag?"

Amelia waved. "You can't save his penis. It's evidence. We can get one another time."

"Sometimes you are smart, Amelia."

"What do you mean sometimes? I'm smart all the time."

"Only Mommy was smart all the time."

"She wasn't smart when she spilled her drink on the wire. She wasn't smart once, and it killed her. I want to be smart all the time."

"I wish you didn't kill Mommy."

"I made one mistake. Let's not talk about it. I'll try not to make any more mistakes."

"We're all sad Mommy's dead. You'll be sadder if I'm in jail and you're in reform school," I said.

"I don't want to go to school," said Helene.

"You don't want to go to a reform school. It is worse than a regular school. I read a book about reform schools," said Amelia.

"Officer Dickens deserved to die," I said. "I'm not sure if we should kill more people."

Both girls muttered something.

"Helene, I'm taking Amelia with me, because she knows how to make herself cry. If Ivy starts to wake up, stroke her head. Tell her to go back to sleep."

Helene nodded.

"Don't worry. If we do this right, it will be over in an hour."

"I'm still hungry. May I please have another piece of cake first?" asked Helene.

"Take the last piece. You've been such good girls that I'm going to take you to Wetson's for hamburgers and french fries."

"I have always wanted to go there. Helene, do a good job so we go to Wetson's instead of reform school," said Amelia.

"Daddy, if we go to reform school, I want you to come there and kill all my teachers," said Helene.

"Don't forget my teachers," said Amelia. "We might not be in the same school."

I sighed. "I promise to kill your teachers if you go to reform school."

Amelia yanked my head down to kiss me. "Thank you! Mommy was right. You are the best Daddy in the world."

"Mommy was always right," said Helene. "Except she made one mistake." She imitated Sara, looking down and shaking her head.

"You made a mistake. We're not supposed to talk about Mommy," said Amelia.

"I'm sorry. I miss Mommy."

"We all miss Mommy. I know Amelia is sorry. What good would it do to send her to reform school? She wouldn't have good teachers and she would be miserable until she was eighteen."

"Eighteen? I thought I would stay there for a month. A month isn't bad. I could learn new ways to kill people from the other students," said Amelia.

"Forget it. I will be getting extra money from Mommy's life insurance. We're going to live on the Upper West Side of Manhattan. You're going to learn nice things from the students in modeling school."

"I'm going to modeling school?"

"Yes. Helene will go to music school. An hour or two a day, with kids who will never go to reform school."

"None of them?"

"We have to get going. Are you ready, Helene?"

"I'm ready. I want to go to Wetson's soon. Everyone wants to go to Wetson's, especially when it's their first time," said Helene.

I wasn't sure what I would say when we entered the security office. Men are usually nice to another man with a crying kid, excuse me, pre–teen. I was proud of Amelia, she seemed hysterical. Officer Ferguson, Dick's replacement, wanted to get away from us as soon as possible.

Helene was next to the air conditioner, screaming, when we opened the door. I picked up Helene as Ivy sat up. I said, "Ivy! What happened to you? What did you do to my wife?"

"Yeah. Why did you kill her?" said Amelia.

Helene screamed, "She killed my Mommy!"

I said, "Stop!" I put the girls down and pointed to Dick. "Wait. Ivy, did he rape you?"

Ivy's scream hurt my ears. Officer Ferguson approached us. "There's no need for two children to see this."

I squeezed Helene's shoulder when she started to speak.

"I am sorry about your wife. You were not involved.

Get out of here. Take your kids to Wetson's, down the block. Get out of the hotel for a couple of hours.

Stop at the desk and tell them to give me the number of your new room. You will have papers to sign. I can bring them over later."

I held my daughters, to avoid shaking his hand. "Thank you. Wetson's is a great idea." I pointed to Amelia, nodded toward Sara's medical bag and said, "Don't forget your purse." Amelia carried the bag by its handles.

On the elevator, Amelia asked, "Can I hold Mommy's bag?" I told Helene, "You can hold it later." I adjusted the straps for her sister.

"Daddy, I would have forgotten the bag," said Amelia. "You can be the Boss as long as you're alive. Mommy told me you were smart. Helene, is this okay with you? I thought about it. He's smarter than us. He can help us kill more people."

Helene's evil grin returned. "Daddy can be the Boss, because I would like to kill more people. I would like to kill someone all by myself. But I want you and Daddy to be there, in case I have a problem."

Amelia raised her arms for me to pick her up. "I'm glad I have a smart sister. I'm glad you're here, so I won't have to go to reform school.

But sometimes I feel like the stupidest person in this family. It's not a good feeling. Do you think I am the stupidest person here?"

I kissed Amelia. "You know more stuff than Helene, because you're older."

Helene said, "It doesn't bother me."

"You're not supposed to know everything," said Amelia.

Helene looked down and shook her head. "Only Mommy knew everything. She didn't know one thing, and it killed her. I miss Mommy."

"You don't know everything. We're not supposed to talk about Mommy. Daddy, this is a hard day for me," said Amelia.

I hoisted Helene on my other arm. I held them by putting my thumbs through my empty belt loops. On the elevator, I said, "We're not done. Hold on to me. I want to carry both of you, as long as possible. People are less likely to bother me if I am holding two little kids."

Helene pinched my cheek. "Don't call us little kids."

"Sorry. Everyone thinks you are ordinary children."

"I have to think of a way to make myself look shorter, so I can do this as long as possible," said Amelia.

"All the girls will be tall in modeling school."

"I won't be the tallest? I stopped being a girl today. I'm a murderer. It's not nice to kill people. But it's a lot of fun. I don't feel bad about doing it."

"I promised Mommy I would be a Doctor. I don't mind being a Doctor. I would like to be a surgeon to look inside people without getting in trouble. I wish Mommy was here to help us. Mommy would kill anyone who wanted to send us to reform school," said Helene.

"I don't know if she would have killed them," I said. "Mommy would have made their life miserable,"

"We should dedicate our next murder to Mommy. She would be proud of us," said Amelia.

Helene said, "Daddy, is murder educational?"

I avoided answering her question as I carried my daughters to the front desk. I put them down on the counter, my technique for speedy service. A male clerk, with "Alvin" printed on his name tag, accepted my room key.

"Hello Alvin. We have a problem. Can you please transfer us from 612? The police will be there soon. Please give our new room number to the police, and Officer Ferguson."

Alvin handed me a key. "I'm sorry. Take 624 down the hall. Is there anything else?"

"Yes. I would like to reserve a babysitter for 6 PM tomorrow."

Helene said, "Make sure she knows how to read *Snow White*."

Amelia added, "She must be able to read all the characters in different voices. We want a professional babysitter who will do a good job."

Alvin said, "That's an interesting request, little girl. Let's see who is available tomorrow."

Amelia reached over to punch his shoulder with her left hand. She said, "I'm not a little girl."

Amelia removed Sara's bag, got down and walked around the counter. She grabbed the end of the clerk's tie, and pulled him down a couple of inches. She said, "I want to know if I am taller than you," before she released him.

"Excuse me! Guests are not allowed to be in this area," said Alvin.

"Daddy, is Amelia going to kill him?" asked Helene.

An older woman laughed and walked over to the disturbance.

Amelia pointed to the laugher. "Be quiet. Don't treat me like a little kid. I'm here to see if I'm taller than Alvin."

"How did you know my name?"

"Sheesh! First you think I'm a little kid, now you think I can't read."

Amelia turned to the now–quiet laugher, who approached us. Amelia looked at her name tag. "Hi Leslie. I'm Amelia. You seem smarter than him."

Leslie smiled. "I'm his supervisor."

"Good. Please help me with something. Who's taller?"

Amelia stood with her back next to Alvin.

"He is. It's close," said Leslie.

"Alvin, take off your shoes. I want to see if you have anything in them to make you taller," said Amelia.

Alvin appealed to Leslie, "Do I have to do this?"

"Alvin, take a break. Amelia, please walk to the other side of the counter. I want to show you something."

Leslie returned with her wallet. She removed a photo and placed it on the counter. "You remind me of my daughter Carol. A hit and run driver killed her last year. Police never caught them."

"Please find out who did it. My sister and I will kill them for you," said Amelia.

Leslie patted the top of her head. "You are a sweet girl. You remind me of Carol. She wanted to be a surgeon. Carol was always catching bugs and dissecting them."

Helene patted Leslie's hand. "I would like to look inside Carol's killer. I would like to do it while he is alive, because it will be more interesting."

Leslie smiled at my daughters. "You are fascinating children. I know your father is nice from the way you behave. I am sure you have a wonderful mother."

"My wife died tonight," I said.

Leslie walked around the counter. She hugged me while I cried.

Helene tapped my leg and handed me a tissue. "Please stop crying. Please marry Leslie right away. She is nice, and we need a new Mommy."

Helene turned to Leslie. "Daddy is good in bed. Mommy told us before she died."

"You're not supposed to tell her now. She's supposed to find out later," said Amelia.

"I'm sorry. I didn't know."

"It's about time you didn't know something. I'm glad you're on my side, and not helping the people who want to send me to reform school."

Leslie broke our hug. "Why would anyone want to send either of you to reform school? You're the smartest children I ever met in this hotel."

Leslie smiled at the girls. "And I meet lots of children here."

"If you promise not to call us children, we will let you be our Mommy. I think you would be a good Mommy. Not as good as our old Mommy, but good enough. Would you like to be our new Mommy?" said Helene.

Amelia punched her sister's shoulder. "You didn't ask me. Please marry Daddy soon, so Helene will stop complaining that she misses Mommy."

Leslie laughed and hugged me. I jerked away when I realized I was pressing an erection against her hip.

"I felt you," said Leslie.

"I'm sorry."

Amelia tapped on Leslie's hand. "Did you go to college?"

"I have a degree in Hotel Management from Johnson and Wales College."

Helene tapped her other hand. "Did you ever want to be a nurse?"

"Why would I want to be a nurse? All they do is take orders from Doctors." Leslie smiled. "I make more money than nurses."

Helene pulled a hundred dollar bill out of her pocket. "Money's not important. We have plenty of money. See?"

Leslie gave me a questioning glance. I said, "My mother gives it to them. She's in 618, want to meet her?"

"You're ready to get married," said Leslie. "Good for you. Don't brood over your wife." My erection returned after she stuck her tongue in my mouth.

Leslie pushed me away. "I don't know what got into me. I'm glad the lobby is empty. I could lose my job."

"You don't need a job if you marry Daddy," said Amelia. "Do you play any musical instruments? And do you know anything about modeling?"

Leslie bent over to Amelia, "I had twelve years of piano lessons. I modeled for the Sears catalog when I was your sister's age."

"Why aren't you a model now?"

"I got fat. I lost interest in modeling, after I lost weight."

"You should dye your hair a new color. We can look at magazines until you find the right color. You would look better with a different color," said Amelia.

"This is my natural color. I had red hair when I was your age."

"See what I mean? Models dye their hair. Their mothers should also dye their hair."

"I don't mind dying my hair. I would like to move. Where do you live?"

"We live in Manhattan," said Helene.

Leslie sighed. "I always wanted to live in Manhattan. It's a good thing you've got money. I bet you have a nice place."

She looked at the girls. "But I have a big problem. I have a husband. I can't stand him, but we're married."

"Where is he now? Would you like us to kill him, so he will be dead when you get home? My sister and I will kill him for you if he's not too big. Otherwise, we will tell Daddy to kill him," said Helene.

I almost fainted, then regained enough strength to say, "I don't kill people."

Amelia laughed. "We know you like killing people. It is nothing to be ashamed of."

Leslie forgot about losing her job. She kissed me warmly. "I know you would never kill anyone. I don't know what happened to me. You're a wonderful father."

Helene said, "Mommy said that, before she died."

"Please stop talking about Mommy. You're going to make me cry," said Amelia.

Leslie picked up Amelia. "Please don't cry. I feel like I'm going to cry. I never met anyone like you and your sister. But I still have a big problem."

"We do not want you to be our mother if you have a terrible disease and you're going to die soon. I do not want to lose two mothers in one week, and definitely not on the same day. Please tell us if you are going to die soon, or if it is a different problem," said Amelia.

Leslie put Amelia down. She looked at both girls. "I have a husband. Excuse me."

Two EMTs pushing a stretcher stopped to chat with Leslie. A strapped–down Ivy said, "You did this."

Helene said, "Excuse me?"

"Stop bothering us," said Amelia.

I smiled at Ivy. She said, "I thought it was her. It was you. What do you teach them?"

I leaned over and whispered, "I teach them how to torture babysitters. They're still learning. Don't forget to practice reading *Snow White*, if you want to be their babysitter again."

Ivy let out a blood–curdling scream.

I leaned back as the EMTs returned. One of them said, "Don't pay attention to her. She's hysterical. She killed two people."

"She killed our Mommy," said Helene.

The other EMT said, "She killed your Mommy?" He glared at Ivy. "Thanks for telling me." He turned to the girls, "You won't see her again. She's going to have an accident on the way to the hospital."

Ivy gasped and fainted. "It's easier when they're passed out," he said. Don't worry about a thing."

I felt like giving him a hundred dollars. "There goes the witness," said Amelia.

Helene punched her. "It was bad because Mommy died."

Amelia punched her back. "It can't happen again. I wish you would stop talking about it. Daddy, please marry Leslie. We need a new Mommy."

"Let's eat first."

We returned an hour later. Amelia carried a shopping bag with six boxed meals for children. She walked to the front desk and handed a box to Alvin. "Go eat. Leave us alone. We want to speak to Leslie."

Leslie appeared, looking great, in jeans and a white t–shirt with a red hotel logo. "I have to get going. My husband will beat me if I'm not home in a half hour, with two six packs of beer."

"You let him hit you?" said Amelia.

I tapped Amelia's shoulder. "Not so loud."

Leslie nodded toward the door. We joined her outside and walked halfway down the block. I tried to hug Leslie, but she pushed me away. She put her hands over her face and bawled.

Amelia tapped my hip. "You're the Boss. Please take care of this. I want to eat more room service and Wetson's in our new room. I would also like to watch a movie. No stories tonight."

Leslie wiped her tears with a dirty handkerchief. "I'm all right. He's been angry at me since Carol died. I was supposed to drive her to her friend's house the day she died. But I was tired from working the late shift. I told her to take the bus. At least he doesn't make me have sex. We haven't had sex in over a year."

"You can have sex with Daddy as long as Amelia and I are not in the room. But if you want, I can stay and take pictures with my new camera. Daddy? Can we please go to the gift shop and buy more film?" asked Helene.

Leslie shuddered.

"Please believe me. She's never done this."

Leslie kissed my cheek. "I believe you." She turned to the girls, "And I don't believe you girls killed anyone." She kissed each girl on the cheek. "Children have wild imaginations."

Leslie stuffed her handkerchief into her purse. "I'm a coward. I need a drink to do this. Let's go to your room and have a drink before I call him."

Helene tapped Leslie's leg. "Mommy liked to drink Scotch."

"Helene, why are you torturing me?"

"I'm sorry. I forgot."

Helene broke up my hug with Leslie. "Please don't start sexing in the street. It's not nice. Amelia and I can stay with Grandma tonight. Daddy, do you trust Leslie?"

"We all better trust Leslie if you want me to marry her."

Leslie blushed.

"I will give her my camera. She can take pictures while you are sexing so I can find out what happens."

Leslie giggled. "Where do you learn these things?"

"We read books," said Amelia. "We don't watch TV at home. We only watch TV when we live in this hotel."

Leslie kissed my cheek. "You have amazing children."

"We're not children. We're pre–teens," said Helene.

"I'll remember. I would love to see you every day. How do I get rid of my husband? I can't leave."

"Sure you can. Tell my mother about it. She will pay for a lawyer. Don't call him. He will threaten you. He might scare you into bringing him beer."

Leslie sighed. "You're right. How do you know this?"

"Mommy said Daddy was the smartest person in the world. He knows everything," said Amelia.

Leslie sobbed. "Please have a drink," I said. "Stay with us. I can sleep on the floor."

I waited for Leslie to stop crying. "You don't have to sleep on the floor," she said. "The carpets are filthy, they're only cleaned once a year. I'm not worried about you."

"Are you sure?"

"I'm sure. Let's have a drink and watch a movie with your daughters. I haven't had a drink for a year. I'm afraid to relax at home.

We don't sleep in the same room. I only married him because I was pregnant. I got pregnant at sixteen with Ronald."

"You have a son? Do we have to see him?" said Amelia.

A bitter look crossed Leslie's face. "He's in prison. He's not getting out for twenty five years. He took after his father, not me."

"I'm glad we won't have to share a bathroom with him," said Amelia.

Helene punched Amelia harder than usual. Leslie moved toward her, but I tugged her arm. She relaxed when I put my arm around her shoulder.

Helene told Leslie, "I'm allowed to hit my sister. If you're going to be our new mother, we're going to have to teach you the rules. Ouch!"

Helene shook her hand. "I'm sorry I hit you hard. I had to show our new mother. We're allowed to hit each other. It's okay. We don't mind. Daddy, please remind me not to hit Amelia so hard. I hurt my hand."

I squeezed Leslie's hand. "I'm the Boss and I'm making new rules right now."

"Do we have to do this in the street in front of everybody?" asked Helene.

"Yes. I'm the Boss. We have to do it now."

"These rules better not be complicated."

"They're not complicated."

"I hope they are educational."

Leslie and I separated. I got down on one knee.

"The sidewalk is dirty. You better be careful," said Amelia.

"This is the most wonderful thing I've ever seen," said Leslie.

Amelia and Helene said, "Be quiet!"

Leslie imitated Steve Martin, "Well, excuse me."

"You're not allowed to talk like Mommy," said Helene.

"She didn't know," I said.

"I don't think I know anything anymore," said Leslie.

"It's about time there's someone in this family who is not as smart as me," said Amelia.

I grinned at a surprised Leslie before I presented our new policy.

"Is everybody listening? These are the new rules." I waited for three nods.

"First, there's no more hitting. Helene hurt her hand. What would happen if she couldn't play piano tomorrow, and she had to give a concert?"

Leslie grabbed my shoulder. "She gives concerts? Ouch! What was that? She bit me. Why did she bite me? What did I do?

She gives concerts and she bites people? People she wants her father to marry? Is this going to be dangerous? I can still go home and bring my husband his beer," said Leslie.

"I'm sorry. I didn't bite you hard. I only bit you because my hand hurt and I couldn't hit you," said Helene.

"Why didn't you use your other hand? That's twice you didn't think of something. You're getting stupider, and our new Mommy is going to be smarter than you," said Amelia.

Helene faked tears. She walked over to Leslie and held up her hands. Leslie lifted Helene and sobbed. "Daddy, Leslie is getting me wet. I might get a disease. I don't know her."

"Don't worry, Helene." Leslie broke their hug. "I don't have anything."

Amelia walked over. "Are you sure? Daddy, is the Board of Health open? Please take Leslie there before you start sexing. Ouch! Where did that come from?"

Helene grinned. "I hit you with my other hand." She turned to Leslie, "Why did you get me wet?"

"I haven't held a little girl for a long time. I thought of Carol. She was so much like you."

"Carol wasn't like us, because nobody except Daddy is as smart as us. We want to know about Ronald," said Amelia.

Leslie faced us. "Ronald took after his father. He was always looking for the easy way out. He managed to stay out of trouble until he was thirteen."

Leslie looked queasy. I handed her a cup of juice from our Wetson's bag. She took a sip. "I wish I could have met your wife."

"We do too," said Helene.

"Please finish," said Amelia. "What happened to Ronald?"

Leslie sighed. "We were living in Providence. I was working and going to school. My husband was driving trucks. He only came home once a week. I should have left when he came home with the clap."

Helene interrupted, "Is 'the clap' a disease?"

"It is a disease you get from sleeping with prostitutes," said Leslie.

Amelia laughed. "He wasn't reading *Snow White* to her."

"They were sexing," said Helene.

"I'm not sure if sexing is a word. You can use it until we check the dictionary in the room," said Amelia.

Leslie asked Amelia, "You brought a dictionary with you?"

"Of course. How do you think I learn new words, to be smarter than Helene? It's only a paperback. We have bigger dictionaries at home."

"How many dictionaries do you have?"

"You'll find out later, if Daddy marries you. Please finish the story. I'm still hungry."

I removed four hamburgers from the bag. "I would rather eat tuna and American cheese. Daddy, when we finally get up to our room, I want to order food from room service," said Amelia.

"You carry a dictionary, you've never eaten at Wetson's, and you don't have a TV. No wonder you're smart," said Leslie.

"We don't go to school either. Now please finish. I want to go upstairs and order different food from room service," said Amelia.

Leslie gasped. "I can't believe this. Why don't they go to school?"

Helene smiled. "We're too smart for school. Please finish your story because I have to go to the bathroom."

"Thank you. I will always remember this. I never met people like you." Leslie raised three fingers like a scout. "I promise I will never go back to my husband."

Amelia groaned. "We believe you. Can you please tell us about Ronald now?"

"One more thing," said Helene. "What is your husband's name?"

"Ronald. My son is Ronald Junior." She kissed me and laughed. "I'm glad your name isn't Ronald."

I squeezed Leslie's wet hand, and she continued. "Where was I? Oh, when he was thirteen, he took a joy ride with older kids in a stolen car. The other kids ran away, but not my little genius."

Helene interrupted. "He's not a genius. Only Daddy, Amelia and me are geniuses."

Leslie scowled. "He was nothing like Carol. Ronald spent the next year in reform school."

"Reform school?" said Amelia.

"It's where they send children who are too young to go to jail. Six months later, he got drunk, stole a car by himself, and drove it into a tree. He went back to reform school until he was 18.

My husband got him a job unloading trucks, after reform school. He worked for about a year, and he found a girl friend. Then he got into drugs, PCP."

"I'm sorry to mention Mommy," said Helene. "Mommy didn't know why people took illegal drugs."

"Will you please finish?" said Amelia.

Leslie looked at me. "You know those signs in 7–11 that tell you they only keep 35 dollars in the register?"

I nodded. "Ronald Junior was too high to read them. He doesn't remember robbing a 7–11, or stabbing the cashier."

"It's time for the new rules," I said. "Does anyone have anything to say?"

Leslie raised her hand. "You've given me a new life. I will request a transfer to Manhattan."

"You're living with us. We have a nine room apartment," said Amelia.

Leslie kissed me. "I'm not going back to my husband."

"You might have to see him in court," I said.

Leslie clenched her jaw. "He can't hit me in court."

"Please hurry, Daddy," said Amelia.

"These are the new rules. First, no more punching."

"My hand still hurts," said Helene. It was swollen. I wished Sara could examine it.

"We'll look at it upstairs."

"Wait. Are your parents alive?" said Amelia.

Leslie sighed. "No. My mother died when I was twelve. She had leukemia. It was awful. My father died last year.

He visited Ronald Junior in prison once a week. Dad stopped visiting me because my husband was never nice to him."

Helene patted Leslie's hand. "Daddy promised to kill my husband if he is not nice to me. If my husband acts like your husband, Daddy will kill him. Right, Daddy?"

Leslie kept me from answering, by putting her tongue in my mouth. When I responded a little too well, she patted the bulge in my crotch. "Later, big boy."

"Daddy? Did she touch your penis?"

"It's okay, Amelia. Daddy is going to marry her," said Helene.

I got down on one knee, and held Leslie's hand. "Will you marry me?"

I heard a laugh and saw the bottom of a uniform. Leslie said, "This is none of your business." A Jacksonville Beach policeman said, "Sorry," and continued his patrol.

"Leslie knows how to scare a policeman. She could be helpful," said Amelia.

"I changed my mind. I don't want to kill anyone," said Helene. I'm sorry. You will have to kill people by yourself. I hope you don't mind."

"I know what you mean. The story about Ronald scared me."

My eyes moistened as attendants loaded two covered stretchers into a van. Leslie stepped in front of me to block my view. "They're not supposed to use the front door."

Amelia tapped my hip. "Can we please go inside?"

Leslie stroked my head. "You poor man. I hate to leave you alone. I'll get in trouble, if someone sees me go upstairs in my street clothes.

I'll use the employee entrance and meet you. What room did Alvin give you?"

"624. I have to go to 618. Do you mind meeting my mother?"

"I'm not leaving you alone. Please don't leave me alone. I can still go home and bring him his beer.

You're nice. Amelia reminds me of Carol. How do I know you won't turn into Ronald?"

Leslie wiped her face and laughed. "What happens if you find out that Helene is smarter than me?"

"I'm sorry, there's nothing I can do about it," said Helene.

I laughed until I saw Leslie crying. She stopped and wrung out her handkerchief.

"Please don't do anything disgusting before you marry Daddy. I don't mind being smarter than you," said Helene.

I lifted Leslie's chin to kiss her lips. "I'm not leaving you. We are going in the front door together. We can have a drink, and listen to my mother sing opera."

Leslie smeared her makeup while she wiped her eyes. Amelia handed her a tissue. Leslie said, "You're like Carol. But I don't know if I should be doing this."

"I hope I'm not like Ronald," said Helene.

"You're not like Ronald. Can we please get this over with? I am hungry and I have to use the bathroom." Amelia held Leslie's left hand. "Take her other hand Helene, so we can get moving."

"I will use my good hand," she said.

Leslie stopped when we reached the entrance. Amelia said, "Daddy? May I please be the Boss until we get upstairs? This is taking too long."

Amelia waited for my nod. She said, "Get going! I'm the Boss. You better do whatever I say. Got it?"

The doorman stepped outside. Leslie removed her hand from Amelia's grasp to wipe her nose. Amelia said, "You're not allowed to use this handkerchief until you wash it. It's disgusting."

The doorman chuckled. "What are you laughing at?" said Amelia.

He forced a straight face and opened the door. He asked Leslie, "Are you all right?"

Leslie started crying. "I give up. Daddy, please do something," said Amelia.

I put one hand under Leslie's thighs, lifted her and walked to the elevators.

"I hope I don't lose my job," said Leslie.

"It doesn't matter. We're your Bosses now," said Amelia.

I put Leslie down as the elevator arrived. A bellman, wheeling a cart full of luggage, joined us. He smiled at Leslie. "Hi Joe. This is my new family. These are my daughters, Amelia and Helene. And this is my husband."

Leslie took my hand and looked into my eyes. "Now I know I'm dreaming. I agreed to marry someone without knowing their name."

Helene tapped on Leslie's hip. "Grandma calls him 'Sonny Boy' and that's a nice name. Or you can call him 'Daddy.' He won't mind either name."

I smiled at Leslie. "They called me 'Killer' in High School."

Mother opened the door. "Daddy, why didn't you tell us that you used to be a murderer?" said Amelia.

"I never should have sent you to that school. Who's this? Where did you find her?" said Mother.

"This is Leslie. I met her downstairs. She needs a lawyer to divorce her husband, so we can get married."

"I'm glad you got rid of Sara. She yelled too much."

Helene tapped Mother's thigh. "Grandma, Leslie is not smart. She didn't know Daddy's name."

"He's Sonny Boy. How could you not know that?"

"Now I know I'm dreaming."

The End